FEDERAL PIANIST

Rueful Tales of the Only One

8/31/18

JOHN ROBILETTE

For dear Gil, one of my dearest friends who was always there to help (I needed a lot), even out of trouble. Thanks for your generous and happy presence for the past half century.

John (Jack) Robilette

Teitelbaum Bertrand Publishing

FEDERAL PIANIST

*Dedicated to the memory of the late Richard Boardman, a
Foreign Service Officer who understood all of this.*

CONTENTS

There is nothing more difficult to carry out, nor more doubtful of success, nor more dangerous to handle, than to initiate a new order of things.

— — MACHIAVELLI

The devil said, "All the power of these kingdoms has been given to me, and I give it to anyone I choose. Pay homage to me and it shall be yours."

— — LUKE 4/1-13

FOREWORD

Much of what follows will seem unbelievable, but I do not possess the poetry of notion to have made it all up. Although this book has been made to look like a work of fiction, it is, instead, preponderantly true. Indeed, some of the most outrageous scenes contain dialogue that has been reproduced verbatim. Some scenes have been rearranged or taken out of sequence, and details have been added to heighten interest. In cases where the author was not there, he has relied upon accounts of those who were or recreated the scenes in a way consistent with his personal knowledge of the characters involved and their interrelationships. Those parts that are entirely fictional were the most difficult to write. Names have been changed to protect the parties portrayed, but those involved will probably recognize themselves—then again, they might not.

CHAPTER ONE

*F*or those who believed in signs, it was already portentous. Meteorological reports indicated a high tide on the east coast, a small earthquake in California, and winds ripping through Washington, D.C., carrying dark cloud vapors over the city.

First, a long, large black car pulled up in front of the agency. It was not the regular dark-blue sedan in which cabinet members were routinely driven about. Harry had rented a real limousine instead, and it looked ominous. Even the windows were blackened, which gave it the effect of a fortress or some piece of military equipment. Several men exited the automobile, wearing pinstriped suits and carrying briefcases. Harry's adjutant emerged, a tall, blond man of about thirty with a scar running diagonally across his cheek. Then came Harry, almost springing out of the back seat with a large head on a diminutive sixty-five-year-old body, moving fast through the doors of the agency, the lobby, and into the elevator, followed by the suits and briefcases. People standing around the security desk started whispering about what was in the briefcases.

"Looks like the people who follow the president around with that coded panel for nuclear weapons."

"He's not that high up," said another. "He's only sub-cabinet level. And take a look at that bulletproof raincoat. Who the hell would want to shoot him anyway?"

"I hear it weighs about thirty pounds. He had to be helped out of his chair the other day."

They moved in single file through the corridors with almost military precision. The men behind Harry stayed close to him, as their heels ground into the carpet and the leather cases knocked against their thighs. People in the lawyers' office were still arranging the bar and table of food, in keeping with the quadrennial ritual of welcoming new directors to the agency. Suddenly, their guests breezed through the door as though it were not there.

Harry stopped abruptly, leaving the last two men bumping into each other. An awkward stillness followed until someone with presence of mind thrust a highball into his hand. Harry did not acknowledge the kindness, and this made people tense. Even though he had not yet been confirmed by the Senate, everyone knew it was a certainty since he was the president's closest friend. So what was this new director like? To the bureaucracy, this changing of the guard was a company risk that renewed itself with every national election. But Harry Cone had prepared himself for this moment. All of his life he had read about, and then cultivated the acquaintance of great and famous men. He studied them silently, waiting for a chance to apply their skills of leadership. Even in this flash of an instant, he was going over a mental checklist: establish yourself quickly, let them know who you are, and, above all, be decisive in giving that first impression.

Suddenly, someone coughed, and twenty-seven people looked at the intruder, then back at Harry. He was ready to begin. But all of his study about power structures had not taken into account that two double scotches at lunch could obliterate the effect of such a moment. Indeed, the sheer power and executive authority of his delivery was lost in the syntax.

"The relevance of my nomination can be threatening only to those whose abortion of the values of the trailblazers of the past can now be relegated to the future—since none of them are here."

One man looked at Harry and cocked his head quizzically. People looked at each other. Someone from the Office of Congressional Liaison focused on Harry's dark, darting eyes and quick movements. "Doesn't he remind you of a rat?" she whispered. "Rattus, rattus." People next to her pretended not to hear but wondered whether this man could really be confirmed by the Senate after all. And the old lawyer, Bradford Ashbury, a recovering alcoholic, stood in the back of the room and said softly, *"Morituri te salutant."* Those who are about to die, salute you!

It was a hot, muggy day—the type eastern Pennsylvania serves up in June. The music department at East Chalmers State University was drawing to a close for the summer, and the little town that cradled it was smothered by humid, still air. Jason Angeletti was a new faculty member in the piano department and had just received his academic baptism by hearing eighty-seven pianists play over the course of three days for their final grade exam. He sat with two other faculty in a large studio as one student after the other came in to perform their jury pieces. Most of them weren't any good. His students were the worst; they couldn't clap in rhythm, probably dance, or even read music very well. As a new arrival, he had been assigned the dregs, those students whom the more long-standing faculty didn't want. So he sat there, biding his time and trying to stay awake while their fingers stuttered on the keyboard, starting and stopping until they wound their way through the piece.

One of the other faculty in the room, who happened to be on Jason's tenure committee, studied his colleague. He watched Jason's spare frame shift in the chair. Everything about him seemed average in appearance. His face was unlined due to his relative youth, and he still had a full head of hair at thirty. But it was hard for him to disguise his lack of interest. Academia was a bleak scene for a young musician who wanted a performance career. It was only a port in the storm, a way to subsidize one's artistic habit and dreams until something better came along, if it ever would.

It was the next morning as he was sleeping heavily in his quiet, air-conditioned bedroom that the phone rang.

"Hey, man! Ernest Rumbolt's playing a faculty piano recital tonight. It's the last event of the year, and we gotta go."

"What's the big deal?" Jason was too tired to talk, but he couldn't hang up on his colleague. Gordon was, after all, a full professor, and Jason didn't even have tenure.

"The big deal," said Gordon, "is that he didn't cancel. You're new, but in the fourteen years I've been here, he's canceled fourteen times. Some of the old-timers say he hasn't played since getting his tenure twenty-six years ago. He's never made a sound, and he makes more money than the rest of us because of seniority. How's that for justice? I wonder what will happen to the pool?"

"What pool?"

"The faculty puts money into a hat every year, and whoever guesses which day Ernest will cancel gets all the money. It's easy to tell. About two weeks before the performance, he

5

starts having back pain, and his complexion turns chalk white. But no one can remember him having gone this long before crapping out. It's D-Day, man! I'll pick you up tonight."

At 7:30 p.m., Dr. Gordon Throckrush, one of twelve piano professors at East Chalmers State University, parked his car under a street lamp and waited.

Jason came bounding down the stairs of his apartment building with a lean grace and energy. He spotted Gordon's silhouette behind the wheel; it was an imposing outline. Dr. Throckrush had acquired a charisma, a way of magnetizing his presence. It was not due to any aristocracy of birth or intellect, but rather to a waft of llama hair he had transplanted into his scalp—an imposing pompadour that folded into and around itself like sand dunes in the Sahara. At first sight, it rendered people speechless.

"I'd better step on it if we want to get a seat. I'll bet the place will be packed."

Gordon's enthusiasm was contagious enough for his passenger to get clammy hands. To Jason, a full piano recital given entirely from memory was a death-defying act—whether his or someone else's. Then he remembered why they were going to this one.

"Isn't it sad that people will be coming tonight, not to hear the music, but to see if he shows up."

"Hey, man! Sometimes that's the most important thing."

All of the parking lots around the auditorium were full, so Gordon double-parked and they both ran inside. There were only a few scattered seats in the back, and they had to climb over people in the rows to get to them.

Somebody said, "Shh," as people looked at their watches. The house lights dimmed, and a spotlight encircled the piano. Ernest Rumbolt had specially ordered the instrument from the factory store in Philadelphia.

"Is that him?" someone whispered.

A solitary figure moved from behind the curtain, becoming partially visible to the right side of the auditorium. A gasp sounded from part of the audience. Dr. Rumbolt stood for a moment in the wings of the stage. His pencil mustache and white evening jacket gleamed in the soft footlights. His lips stretched into a slight smile… and then he canceled. It was his back, he said. Something snapped.

No one backstage believed him, and that made it difficult to find someone to make an announcement.

Vincent Manini, chairman of the piano faculty, stood up in the front row and faced the audience. "Would the entire piano faculty assemble backstage immediately?" Five minutes later he addressed his colleagues.

"We, eh, have a situation," he said with a nervous giggle. "Poor Ernest's back is keeping him from going on tonight.

Someone's got to tell the audience to go home. Any volunteers?"

"Why not you?" said a belligerent voice from the back.

"Because I, uh, personally invited the dean to this concert and—"

"Maybe we could draw straws?" said another voice.

Vincent's eyes scanned the room. "There aren't any straws around here."

A third person asked, "How about getting somebody from another department?"

Ten people shouted, "Yes!"

They went out into the auditorium and found Rupert Milquette, a voice instructor, and brought him backstage.

"But I just can't do this," he protested. "It will be unpleasant and I'm already under treatment for clinical depression."

Ernest Rumbolt came out of his dressing room and said, "*Bonjour*." He knew only a few words in French and German, mostly hello and goodbye, but used the expressions frequently.

"Ernest, please go out there and play." Rupert Milquette's voice was desperate.

Rumbolt backed himself up against the wall and hunched over.

"I will not go out there. My back pain prohibits me from giving a great performance."

"Here, then," said Rupert, fumbling around in his pocket. "Try one of these."

"What is it?" Rumbolt looked suspicious.

"It's one of my antidepressant pills."

"Go ahead. Swallow it!" someone shouted.

Dr. Throckrush raised his voice in protest. "Come on. Get serious. Those pills take six weeks to kick in. I know! I'm on them myself."

Ernest Rumbolt opened his arms and held them aloft, as though giving a benediction. It was a solemn gesture that quieted everyone. Perhaps now there would be some clarification, or even a change of heart. But he only said, *"auf Wiedersehen,"* then turned and limped down the long, linoleum corridor toward the parking lot.

Rupert asked for a glass of water, took one of his pills, and went out to face the audience.

The ride home was quiet until Gordon broke the silence. "It's in the Eastern Corridor, anyway," he said almost apologetically.

"What is?"

"The university. You've got access to everything: Philadelphia, New York, Washington, D.C. You could be in Podunk, man, at a little school in Nowheres-Ville. You know how tough jobs are in classical music. I've got friends from Juilliard who are practically shoveling shit in places with no restaurants and no airports. They're goin' nuts!"

Jason didn't say that he was going nuts, too. This was only the end of his first year at East Chalmers, but he already saw where it was going: isolation and exile on an island of mediocrity. Maybe it was accepted as a given that it happened to everybody in the business except the superstars. He thought about how he had chased the best teachers all over the world —in Paris, London, and Los Angeles; how he had lived in hovels and squeezed money from scholarships, sponsors, and his parents, all toward becoming an artist, a concert pianist. A friend had called it "chasing the Holy Grail." And now, he was at East Chalmers State University. He had a vacant feeling as he wondered what the future might hold.

"A lot of people wanted this job. You had some stiff competition, man." Gordon kept his eyes on the road but read Jason's dismay. Perhaps it was his own as well. Both had wanted a performing career, but neither had achieved their dream. In the toughest of all businesses, teaching was their refuge.

Gordon increased the speed of the automobile as though it could run over the unpleasant thoughts. He rolled up the window to quiet the sudden rush of air and started to turn toward Jason. But large strands of his hair got caught in the window, restricting his movement. He had to roll the window back down to free himself. And when he finally managed to turn his head, the top of his pompadour brushed against the roof of the car, making a grainy kind of sound.

Jason winced. It was like chalk on a blackboard.

"It's still better than the parking lot," said Gordon sheepishly.

Jason knew about the incident in the parking lot—everybody at East Chalmers did. It was a defining moment for Gordon when he finally committed himself to a hair transplant. Until then, he had used massive doses of hairspray and a careful comb-over on the top, with his hair grown on the side to maintain the illusion of fullness. But an October wind had changed all that. A sudden burst of air from the east had caused a glutinous mass of hair, welded together by spray and gel, to stand straight up like a cleaning brush, exposing a smooth floor of skin underneath. It stayed vertical throughout the gust, not even fluttering but standing resolute like a flagpole. A few students witnessed this from the parking lot and giggled about it in the corridors. Soon, everyone was referring to "Gordon's drawbridge," or "the mat." Dr. Rumbolt, who had long ago given himself up to bad jokes, called it, "hair raising."

Jason stared out the window in despair.

"You've got to make a living, man." Gordon continued pressing his case. "You've got to make some compromises to fit into the system. I've had to myself."

Jason knew some of Gordon's compromises involved paying

alimony to three ex-wives, all former students. But Jason was single and still chasing the Holy Grail.

Finally, Gordon pulled out what he thought might be his ace in the hole. "You have some decent students at least?"

"Not really, Gordon. One of them offered me a book to read during her lesson because she hadn't practiced."

"How did you handle that?"

"I told her I couldn't read Spanish and asked her if she had another one with pictures."

"Attaboy. Be nice to them because enrollment's down."

The marble conference room of the Senate Foreign Relations Committee was jammed for the confirmation hearings. The press had set up television cameras and glaring lights, and some reporters were kneeling in front of the dais of senators. They trained their lenses on the table opposite the raised platform where a small man sat with dyed-black hair, his hands folded and resting on the green tablecloth.

"Mr. Cone." Senator Pugwam's voice was dramatic and vibrating. "You first met the president through a school carpool. Is that correct?"

"No, Senator, I would not characterize it that way. Neither the president nor I were in school at the time. It was our children's car pool." Harry grinned.

"But you owned the car, did you not?"

"Not entirely. We both owned one car each. Just a moment, Senator." Harry motioned for another man in a pinstripe suit to come over, and they whispered to each other. "I'm sorry, Senator. I had two cars at that time."

"Do you then think, Mr. Cone, that being associated with our future president in a relationship that revolved principally around carpools qualifies you to be director of a federal agency?"

"Well, Senator, if you had done a little more research, you'd know I've been a successful businessman, I have a law degree, and I have three children, which means I'm not impotent. That ought to mean something in this town." Harry's smile revealed rows of long white teeth.

Senator Pugwam continued. "But do you know anything about public diplomacy or foreign policy, Mr. Cone? This is vitally important since the constituency of the International Cultural Communications Agency is exclusively foreign. Let us take, for example, one of its programs, the agency's English Teaching Program in Africa. What are your views on that?"

"Some of those people down there have brains, and it's our job to rescue them."

There was not a murmur in the room.

"Rescue them from what, Mr. Cone?"

"From their circumstances, Senator. Have you been down there? I have personally journeyed into the darkest part of that continent, and I can tell you it's so damn dark down there that you can't see anything—especially at night... No street lights. Nothing!"

Several senators looked stunned, and another dyspeptic.

"Have you drawn any other conclusions?" one of them stammered.

"Sure. I saw a lot of cars that were stalled on main thorough-fares. I thought at the time, and still do, that our government ought to make an instructional film on how to fix a carburetor, send it down there, and get that country moving again."

"Moving where, Mr. Cone?"

"Anywhere else would be better!" Harry was growing testy but quickly calmed himself. "Listen, Senator, there's a lot of misinformation about that part of the world. I had dinner the other night at an Ethiopian restaurant in the District, and I can tell you, there's no famine over there. They just won't eat that junk."

One senator exhaled into the microphone. It sounded like a seashell that one puts to the ear. Another looked more pained than any patrician could, as though he had seen the face of hell. Senator Pugwam, the chairman of the committee, had his own internal seismograph that was sensitive to all political stimuli. His wily brain ticked off the earthquake damage at about a seven on the Richter scale. Why would the president pick such a man? But reality intruded, and he put away such thoughts. Loyalty was what mattered, and Harry had raised sixteen million dollars for the campaign.

Harry was confirmed that morning, and the die was cast.

When Jason turned in for the evening, he was despondent. He lay awake for a while staring at the ceiling, numb but strangely peaceful inside. He was free of any ambition for the first time he could remember, no inner drive, no looking forward. What would be the point of it anyway? He was stuck. His mind wandered while his eyes traced the rim of the ceiling. Maybe he should get out of music. No, that wouldn't do. He couldn't change who he was; music was his way of life. It had chosen him; that he knew in his deepest self. Sleep came gently, and with it dreams of flying, flying on his own, over rooftops and away from faculty meetings and llama hair. And then he heard applause. He was on stage somewhere, being redeemed. But that ended with the intrusive jangling of the telephone; it was morning already.

"Mr. Harry Cone calling from the International Cultural Communications Agency in Washington. Please hold."

Jason froze, as he always did whenever Harry called. He never could relate to him. It had been ten years since those piano lessons, and Jason had never taken them seriously anyway. It was for pocket money, and he was amazed Harry was still caught up with them.

Suddenly, a voice broke through the receiver like the whir of a motorboat. "Jason, boy, what are you up to? I haven't talked to you in a while."

"I'm okay, thanks." Jason was wide awake now. He always was when he dealt with Harry.

"I've still got the music that we used during those piano lessons. And your markings on the score are still helpful."

Jason tensed up. Poor Harry. He never practiced but always thought he was improving. It was like working with P.T. Barnum. And then there was the steady stream of jokes, Harry's one-liners from the Catskills given copiously throughout the lessons. Jason had most of them memorized by now.

"How'd the inaugural thing go?" Harry plunged into Jason's thoughts like a diver into cold water.

"It was a hoot." *The hell it was*, he thought. It was painful to recollect. He felt like he'd finally made it when he received the invitation to play at one of the inaugural festivities. Harry had made the invitation possible in his capacity as chairman of the Presidential Inaugural Committee. He was a close friend of the new president.

Jason remembered walking up the staircase of the National

Portrait Gallery in his tuxedo, past the Gilbert Stuart painting of George Washington. The concert grand piano had been roped off on the second floor under a picture of Calvin Coolidge.

"May I try it?" he asked a woman in a museum uniform.

She nodded, and he played some chords. It was an excellent instrument. He looked around for audience seats, but there were none.

"Is there a place to rest before the performance?"

"This is the performance," she said.

"But those were just a few chords."

"Well, I'm sure people enjoyed them."

"There aren't any people here."

"There will be. The jazz pianist just finished, and now it's your turn."

The woman walked some distance away and stood waiting under a portrait of General George Custer. Two young men with ponytails came in. They removed their shoes and sat on the floor Indian style, with their legs crossed. The woman in the uniform nodded at Jason, and he nodded back. They kept nodding at each other until she took on a stern look. It was time to begin.

After the opening Bach partita, the audience grew to four but never got any bigger. When it was over, the woman from the museum came and leaned over the piano.

"The second performance will start in a few minutes."

"But there were only four people here for this one."

"They're all taxpayers," she said.

The two men with ponytails stayed for the second performance. Their numbers were augmented by three other people: Jason's parents and his teacher, all of whom had flown in for the event.

When he finished, his mother told him he looked nice in his tuxedo.

"I could have worn shorts," he said.

He listed the performance on his résumé, hoping whoever read it had not been there.

"What are you doing now anyway?" Harry was relentless. "If you're free, why not come to LA or Washington, or wherever, and give me a piano lesson?"

"I'm teaching—"

"Teaching?" Harry savored the word as though it were some delicacy.

"Yeah, teaching in a menagerie. You know, academia and that kind of thing."

—

"Academia, huh. Then you're dealing with squirrels, but I'm dealing with lions and tigers." There was a swishing sound on the line, like air pressure being released in short spurts. It was Harry's mouth spray which he used incessantly. Jason wondered if he still dyed his hair black.

"I've read about that—about you, I mean." Jason didn't say what he had read were criticisms in the press of how Harry had handled the inauguration.

"That's all behind me now, boy." Harry's voice had a cutting edge. "We move on in life. Always forward. But it sure has been exciting."

It was clear to Jason that Harry took his notoriety as a compliment.

Suddenly, Harry dropped a *non sequitur*. "And by the way, Jason, do you know why Jewish men die before their wives?"

Here it comes, thought Jason, *waves of them*. "No, why?"

"Because they want to!"

Jason wondered if all power-driven men liked "corn." He decided to short-circuit it. "And they sleep in separate beds... hers is in New York, and his is in Florida."

Harry laughed politely but then stopped. That joke was from his repertoire, so he changed tone. "On a serious note, and this one would be on about a high G, the president has asked me to head up the ICCA. Do you know what that is, Jason?"

"No, sir." Jason added the "sir" after he heard the word "president."

"Every cultural attaché in every American embassy in the world reports to me."

"Wow," said Jason dutifully. Privately, he pitied anybody who worked for Harry. They would have to deal with his hair-trigger temper.

"Why don't you go take a look at that building, Jason."

"What building?"

"The ICCA building."

"Take a look at the building?"

"Yeah."

"Where is it?"

"Somewhere on Pennsylvania Avenue."

"What should I do after I look at it?"

"Report back to me."

"Report what?"

"Whatever you saw."

"I imagine I will have seen a building."

"Right."

"Do you want me to go into the building?"

"Only if you have to come in out of the cold."

Jason could imagine Harry smiling after the last remark. A sort of swagger with his head—from side to side, with a toothy grin. Jason waited a moment and then spoke. "But it's July."

"So what?"

"So there's no need to come in out of the cold." This time Jason smiled.

Suddenly, there was silence.

"That's your opinion," barked Harry. "Look, if you're not interested, then don't go and look!" Harry put the phone down abruptly as he was finishing the last word.

Jason thought, *Well, that's that, another phone call from Harry.* They came intermittently over the years, and Jason could never figure out how Harry kept tracking him down. But when Harry did call, there was always some drama— like a Hollywood spectacular. After all, Harry used to be a Hollywood agent before he made millions with his chain of funeral homes. Jason thought the calls were fun though. It always seemed Harry was about to change Jason's life in exchange for a piano lesson. But it never quite happened. This call was another wash.

The dog days of summer settled over East Chalmers State University. Classes were over and June had turned into July; the air wasn't moving. A blanket of moisture had created a languor that quenched any ambition. Jason was so listless; he wasn't even practicing the piano. Harry Cone's phone call had already been two long weeks ago and there had been no excitement since, so he mostly slept. It was midmorning as he lay in bed trying to remember his dream, when the phone rang. It was a funny ring, slightly off pitch, so he let it ring several times, trying to decide if it was broken. His curt "hello" was met by the cool neutrality of a professional secretary.

"This is the International Cultural Communications Agency calling. Please hold for Dr. Marvin Mariah from the Bureau of Intercultural Exchange."

Jason sat up in bed. *Who in the hell is that?* he wondered.

"Mr. Angeletti, Director Cone asked me to call you." The man's voice was icy but decisive, set in a sort of monotone. "He wants to know if you've taken a look at that building yet."

"What is it that you do, Mr., uh, Dr. Mariah?"

"I'm acting Associate Director designate of the Bureau of Intercultural Exchange at the International Cultural Communications Agency. I'm the Number Three Man, equivalent to Assistant Secretary of State."

To Jason, those were a lot of words.

"Now, back to my original question, Mr. Angeletti. Have you taken a look at the building yet?"

"No, I haven't."

"And may I ask, why not, sir? That was a direct request from Mr. Cone."

"Because I've seen buildings before, Dr. Mariah. I didn't feel it would be productive to look at another one."

"I don't think you understand. The expression 'taking a look' is code in the government for 'seeing what's available.'"

"What's available?"

"A job, Mr. Angeletti… a job! You're a friend of Mr. Cone, right? That puts you ahead of the game in this town because he's the president's closest friend."

Jason's mind swirled. A job? The president's closest friend? He thought back to those damn lessons at Harry's house. He remembered meeting the then governor's children. They were part of a parade of famous people who Harry started introducing Jason to once he sensed his teacher's boredom with the lessons. There were peripheral celebrities and children of this one and that. Then, one day, these kids were trotted out.

"Governor's a friend of mine," said Harry, pointing to them.

So what, thought Jason. Harry still couldn't play that Chopin waltz. Jason's thoughts were jarred by the steely tone of Marvin Mariah's voice.

"Friends are important, you know."

"Who's your friend, Dr. Mariah?"

"I don't discuss who my godfather is with anybody. Information is power in this town, Mr. Angeletti. But since I am speaking on a secure line, I will give you a tidbit. The Foreign Service has already killed Harry's proposal regarding you, so we've got to start from scratch."

It was a violent word, "killed." And what proposal was he talking about? Jason stammered, "What do you mean?"

"Director Cone wrote a memorandum to the heads of the various geographic areas, and it concerned you. Didn't you receive a copy?"

"No."

"Well, I have a copy right here. Let me read it to you:

Memorandum from: Harry Cone, Director, ICCA

To: Area Directors of Asia, Europe, Southeast Asia, and the American Republics.

It is my considered opinion that Jason Angeletti is a monumentally talented American musician of incomparable learning, mesmeric capacities, and far-reaching potential. I myself have been the recipient of his inimitable and illimitable knowledge and vast resources as together we stormed the impregnable quadrilateral of scales, arpeggi, octaves, and repertoire. I believe it is in the best interests of all fifty states that make up this great republic to place their entire arsenal of resources behind this young man in the furtherance of peace and public diplomacy.

Jason rolled his eyes. *Ole' Hollywood Harry*, he thought. "Well, if that's what they killed, Dr. Mariah, then it's just as well. I have no intention of running for office."

"Again, you don't seem to understand, sir. What Director Cone was saying is that the Foreign Service, who man our embassies abroad, should arrange to send you around the world playing concerts and representing the United States."

Suddenly, Jason was more alert than he had ever been in his life.

"That's what was killed," said Mariah.

Jason stopped breathing. Something he had dreamed about all his life, was put within his grasp and then withdrawn, all within seconds. "Why?" he asked, trying to mask his desperation.

"Because the Foreign Service thinks that since you're not famous, you might not be any good. They already think Harry's not any good. He played at a big agency party a couple weeks ago. There was a piano and everything. He did not do you proud, sir."

Jason didn't care how Harry had played. "Tell me, if Harry Cone says he wants me to play around the world, and orders the Foreign Service to arrange it, how can they say no if Harry's their boss?"

"A variety of ways, but they all spell sabotage. That's why I've had my new apartment swept for bugs. And every night after hours, I have all the political appointees who work in my bureau come to my office for a special meeting. The purpose is to trade information on career bureaucrats, the 'lifers,' as we call them."

"Have you had your office swept, too?"

"No need. There isn't a microphone that could pick up anything over the sound of my paper shredder. Listen, Mr. Angeletti, the moment you enter this building, your friends and enemies will already have been made."

"I thought this was a cultural agency, with exchanges and stuff like that. It sounds more like the CIA."

"It is a cultural-exchange agency, but it's also an executive agency that reports directly to the White House. That makes it hardball."

"You're pretty forthcoming with information for someone who doesn't like to give it away."

"Mr. Angeletti, the plans are to bring you in as a political appointee. That means that you're automatically going to be my friend."

Jason's mind was racing. This could be his way out of East Chalmers, but what the hell was he getting into? Were those silly piano lessons he gave Harry on another coast when he was a graduate student going to save him, open new doors? He had to think. What would he do in the government? Maybe it would be exciting for a while, more than the university and its politics. But did he really want to work for Harry? He tried to put things in perspective. Yes, Harry had a bad temper, was ruthless and intimidating. But there were also redeeming factors. Aside from his consuming passion for the piano, Harry had a fondness for children, small dogs, people who had lost fortunes, and pleasant memories of himself. But Jason had to work the music angle into it somehow.

"What would I do, Dr. Mariah? I'm a musician, you know. If I were to consider working at the ICCA, my job would have to have something to do with music."

"We won't worry about that. The deputy director of the agency is bringing in a tuba player from Chicago. He's a friend of his sister or something, so we'll find a place for him. Hey, we won the election, Mr. Angeletti, so all things are possible!"

Jason noticed Marvin Mariah had the same habit as Harry. He hung up the phone as he was saying the last word of the sentence. It was the strangest conversation Jason had ever had.

It was early in the morning. He had forgotten to unplug the phone and cursed the shrill ring when it woke him up. He lay there for a moment in a kind of trance. The phone wasn't broken after all; that was good news. But who was at the other end this time?

"Hey, man, it's Gordon Throckrush. What's up?"

"I'm glad it's you, Gordon." Jason needed someone to talk to. "Some things are turning my life upside down."

"Then we have to talk. How about lunch at Leland's Sports Bar?"

Jason got there first and took a table in a corner. He studied the people at the bar—motorcyclists, and men with tractor hats —and wondered why Gordon had picked the place.

"The food's great!" he said when he arrived. "Try the meatloaf with honey mustard."

But Jason wanted to try a different table since everybody seemed to be looking at them. He made up some excuse, and they moved across the room.

"That's the reason," said Gordon.

"What?"

"We were sitting under the television set. That's why they were all looking at us."

"Well, then why are they still looking at us?"

Jason looked at Gordon's hairdo; he had combed it differently today. It looked like a mountain of mashed potatoes. But he decided not to pay attention. Instead, he launched into his new job prospects.

Gordon gasped. "You mean you're going to become a government spook!"

"That'll never happen. I'd never become like the rest of them."

"Of course you will. If you go there, you'll become like them. You're a hell of a musician and an artist. How can that ever translate into being a spook?"

"You make it sound like the CIA or something."

"Well, isn't that what you said?"

"No. I said the ICCA."

"Same thing, man. It's all the same, a bunch of spooks."

The next morning, Jason was listening to a *nocturne* by Fauré. It played softly through the stereo speakers and could scarcely be heard above the whir of the air conditioner. Suddenly, the phone rang with a peculiar off-pitch ring. He picked up the receiver, thinking he should really get it fixed.

"Please hold for Dr. Rollie Lovemore from the International

Cultural Communications Agency. Oh, is this Mr. Jason Angeletti?"

Jason was transfixed by the voice. It didn't have the cold, sexless, immunity from all feeling that characterized the other secretaries. There was an alluring quality.

"Who wants to know?" he asked, trying to prolong the moment.

"Oh... I'm nobody, Mr. Angeletti. Not nearly as important as you are."

"Why?"

"Because everyone here knows who you are. You're a friend of Mr. Cone's, and he thinks you're a great artist. I couldn't compete with that." Her voice had the sultry purr of a kitten who was nestling her master, awakening him to the new day.

Jason stammered, "But even an artist needs friends. Tell me your name."

"Marilyn."

"Is there more?"

"Marilyn Goodrump," she sighed. "Now let me pass you on to Mr. Lovemore, or I'll get in trouble." She trumped her exit with a breathless coo, "Please!"

There was a sudden crackle on the line.

"Hello, I'm Rollie Lovemore, acting associate director of the Bureau of Intercultural Exchange here at the ICCA."

Jason blinked. He blurted, "Is Marilyn Goodrump as good-looking as her voice?" He regretted it immediately.

There was a silence at the other end, then a soft chuckle. "I've never actually seen her voice, but she's a very nice person. Now, may we get down to business?"

Jason tried to refocus. "What ever happened to the other guy that was acting in the same job you are, Dr. Mariah?"

"He's no longer with the agency."

"Why not?"

"The director relieved him the day before his confirmation hearings. I can assure you, Mr. Angeletti, that I do not intend to handle things the way he did."

"What happened?"

"Marvin Mariah made an end run around the director. He couldn't get his way on something, so he went right to the White House. I would never be that disloyal in the chain of command. But what really did him in was when he requisitioned a shoulder holster from the Bureau of Administration and Personnel."

"Has any of that affected my situation?"

"Frankly, it has made it more difficult to bring you in. Dr.

Mariah leaked a memo that the director wrote about you. The newspapers have it, and we're worried about the piano-teacher angle."

"What do you mean?"

"That Harry Cone is bringing his piano teacher on board. It doesn't look good. But don't worry; we'll still do it somehow. How fast it can be done is another matter. That may depend on how badly Mr. Cone needs a piano lesson."

Jason gripped the phone hard when he heard Rollie Lovemore's soft chuckle.

"So just hang on, Mr. Angeletti, and I'll have somebody get in touch with you shortly. I would never handle this the way Dr. Mariah did. If you talk to the director in the near future, I would appreciate if you would tell him that."

It was a full week before that funny ring sounded again. This time, the phone was under a pillow, which created a muffled sound.

"Hello, I'm Ed Stanley, director of the Office of Performing and Visual Arts. Dr. Lovemore asked me to call. I've been looking into this job thing carefully, and I really think you're better off just filling out a one seventy-one form and going through regular channels here."

"So you're in his bureau?"

"No, I'm actually in another bureau."

"Then why is he having you call me?"

"Because I've got the arts stuff."

"What's he got?"

"The culture stuff."

"Isn't art the same as culture?"

"I don't get into that."

"What do you get into?"

"The arts stuff."

"Why can't Harry just hire me? Why do you want me to go through the system? Anybody could do that."

"The director could hire you, but then you'd be a political appointee instead of a career person."

"What's the difference?"

"If you're political, you have to leave when he does. If you're career, nobody can fire you."

"What do the career people do, anyway?"

"The arts and culture stuff and some information stuff."

It seemed to Jason that every phone call brought out a new

character. If this last one was the most ineffective, then Rollie Lovemore was the most disingenuous. Rollie had obviously shifted his responsibility to this new guy in order to get off the hook. Mr. Stanley wasn't even in Rollie's bureau, didn't have the power to hire, and suggested a routine path that a voice over a recording at the agency could have given him. Jason thought Harry might want him hired, but there were others who didn't. He wondered how Harry was faring, if he was surrounded by people like this. And what other kinds were there?

Mark Leduk sat at his desk and adjusted his French cuffs. Then he looked into a small mirror and moved his palm back across the hair on his temples. Everything was in place; he was ready to perform, to take Harry over to the Bulgarian embassy. There was nothing to be nervous about. He had broken in countless new directors before, and this would be a simple ceremony where nothing could go wrong. Maybe Harry Cone was nuts, but Mark had worked with those types before. He felt confident about making the spoils system work for him. After all, he had already gained Harry's confidence by explaining to him the difference between the counsel, the counselor, the consulate, and the general consul.

He looked in the mirror again and liked what he saw: the consummate professional bureaucrat and a romantic hero to the entire Foreign Service Corps. He enjoyed planting the stories that abounded concerning his professional and personal life: the time in Budapest when he escaped the communists; or in Tanganyika when he did the Bali dance under a pole while balancing a shot of Cognac on his forehead. He got up from behind his desk and buttoned his double-breasted blazer, then fluffed the handkerchief next to the lapel. As he walked slowly through the suite of offices reserved for the counselor to the agency, he took pride in the sheer number of people who worked for him; his staff even rivaled the director's. He began his personal procession to the elevators and down to the lobby and the waiting limousine. He strutted a bit because that's how he felt, small in appearance but big in stature. He was a career minister by act of Congress—the highest of the high in the Foreign Service. A smugness pervaded him, a self-love that was against all available evidence to the contrary.

"What am I supposed to do there, anyway?" said Harry, as the car sped toward the embassy.

Mark opened the fiberglass window that separated the passengers in the backseat from the driver. "Could you close the window on the director's side, please? It's making a draft on him." He turned toward Harry. "First things first." Then he bit his lip and looked out the window as though lost in thought. "Mr. Director, your question is an excellent one and deserves an answer. Bulgaria is a communist satellite of the Soviet Union; therefore, we cannot hope to have any meaningful political dialogue. But after you sign this agreement, we will have a new cultural accord, which is at least a foot in the door

—a step toward improved relations. So, after you simply sign on the appointed line, there will be a champagne reception afterward with NATO and Warsaw Pact ambassadors."

Harry kept drumming his fingers on his knee as though his leg was a keyboard.

"You know, Mr. Director, that I also love music."

Harry turned toward Mark Leduk, suddenly showing an interest.

"Yes, indeed, Mr. Director. I used to vacation in Salzburg, Austria, so that I could drink in the same atmosphere as that great genius, Wolfgang Amadeus Mot-zachh-rtt." There was a little rattle of phlegm and spray of saliva.

Harry took out his handkerchief and wiped his face. Even though he had never met an Austrian, he knew instinctively it was not pronounced that way.

At the embassy, the Bulgarian ambassador began the simple ceremony with welcoming remarks and a toast to the spirit of cultural cooperation between the two countries. As the official photographers' cameras flashed bulbs, and the distinguished guests raised their crystal glasses, Harry strode briskly to the center of the rotunda.

"Mr. Ambassador, I have a few brief remarks."

Mark Leduk's eyes narrowed. He knew of no such remarks.

"I have brought you something which is very special to me."

Harry held aloft a book that had been cradled in his arm. "I would like you to have this, and I have written an inscription on the inside cover. This book, Mr. Ambassador, is about the Statue of Liberty and tells of the teeming millions of immigrants who came to this country escaping tyranny and repression from countries such as your own."

Mark Leduk had always prided himself on being a hardened veteran. Before this moment, he could never have imagined having trouble with his bowels. Every ambassador standing near him was somewhat less involved, and managed to stop their glasses in midair on the way to their next sip. It was as if in one frozen moment, they had all contracted lockjaw.

The next morning, Mark Leduk quietly closed the door to his office and made some calls on his private line. They were to the heads of the five geographic areas, powerful men in the machinery of the agency and many of them protégés of Mark. All were senior-level Foreign Service Officers.

There was complete silence. The Foreign Service knew this was a dangerous game. They also knew that if Harry sensed anything, he would retaliate. Even though he could not fire them because they were career employees, he could transfer them to a post overseas that might break them. At Ouagadougou on the Upper Volta, the isolation would be complete, or he could send them to a hardship post with its disease and physical danger. Then the old nemesis of the corps —alcoholism of one or the other spouse—might surface, with alienation soon to follow.

But Pierre LaRue, director of the European area, also had a devastating weapon, one that he and his colleagues had used well in the past. "I have a memo here," he said. "We could leak it to the press."

"What is it?" someone asked.

"It's from Harry Cone and lists rules and regulations for his official travel. It's all of a personal nature: insuring his airplane seat is sufficiently distanced from the bathroom in first-class air travel so that he won't hear any flushing; that he must never be left alone in a crowd lest he seem unimportant; and absolutely no one should smoke in his presence."

Everybody laughed because this was the kind of stuff that Washington did not like. It might just start the ball rolling in suggesting that Harry was a liability to the new president.

Another area director suggested wiring a major article on Harry in the *Washington Post* that would take him apart in print, if, in fact, Harry didn't witlessly take himself apart first.

"Harry's guileless about Washington," Pierre said. "He'll probably agree to the interview to blow his own horn. But we'll have to make sure the press section at the agency doesn't find out about the interview in advance and kill it."

"I can arrange that," said another officer.

The meeting was over before dessert was served.

It was toward the end of the month when two articles appeared in *The Washington Post*—back to back, like a one—two punch. The first concerned rules for traveling that Harry had given his staff, which made him seem like a spoiled *pasha*. But the second article was far more damaging and appeared on the cover of the prestigious Style section of the paper. The photograph made him look like Rasputin, and he managed to sound at once silly and bellicose during the luncheon interview. He said there were too many people of a particular political persuasion who worked for him. They knew who they were, and they were all marked for destruction. In answer to what he missed about California, he said, "All the beautiful people," and when asked what he thought about Washington, he replied, "Please, not while I'm eating!"

Naturally, none of it went over very well in town. Finally, Harry got a call from someone on the White House staff reminding him that his job was supposed to be low profile. This was not good. Harry decided it was time to see the chief.

As his limousine passed through the marine guard station just off Pennsylvania Avenue, it did not stop or even slow down. Harry was the only man in Washington who was not to be checked or stopped at any point in the White House. He even had clearance to go directly into the living quarters. Everyone knew him, and security throughout the compound had his photographs. The car stopped at the North Portico, and Harry bounded up the steps into the old mansion.

People nodded at him as he wound his way through the rooms and around the old corridors with their overhanging chandeliers, then back outside to the Roosevelt walkway. When he came to the Oval Office in the West Wing, the door was open. He stepped onto the blue rug bearing the presidential eagle, nodded toward the marine guard, and stuck his head inside. "Two flies were flying around and one fly said to the other, 'Hey fly, your man's open!'"

The president threw back his head in laughter. "Harry, it's been too quiet around here. Don't know what I'd do without your jokes. Say, is it true that your wife said she had all these electric gadgets around the house and nowhere to sit down, so you bought her an electric chair?"

Harry laughed dutifully. "Did you know that her mother willed her body to science, but science is contesting the will?"

The president exploded with a belly laugh, then slammed his open palm down on the desk. His whole upper torso seemed to gyrate. A tall man, he appeared in good physical condition for his age, with a barrel chest, wide shoulders, and dyed hair. He caught his breath and looked at Harry. "Your wife told mine that the article in the *Post* really bothered you." The president was still panting. "That it didn't come out the way you wanted. Well, I've had that happen to me plenty of times, so don't worry about it. It's like being over fifty. The best thing about it is you don't have anything left to learn the hard way."

Harry didn't get it but laughed anyway. It was his turn now, but he couldn't think of a joke. He didn't need one; he had already gotten what he came for.

During the ride back he decided there were too many land mines in this city. He had trouble operating the way he wanted. Also, he was tired, and there was no opportunity for rest. He had to find something to transport himself, to touch that tired spot way down deep. He needed a renewal. He told his driver to pull over and "get it out of the trunk."

The man pulled onto a side street, opened the trunk, and removed a long, narrow wooden box that resembled a small coffin. He carried it to Harry in the backseat and carefully placed it over the director's lap.

Harry opened the lid and looked at the black and white keys. They seemed to smile. He was glad he had specially ordered this dummy keyboard from Steinway. He started to move his fingers over the keys, and even though there was no sound, the tactile sensation relaxed him while the car moved smoothly back onto Pennsylvania Avenue. He started playing a tune he had learned in his youth, but the bass line had always troubled him. He worked his left hand while he imagined the sound in his mind and snapped his right hand to the rhythm. Then he started to hum, and finally, ever so softly, his baritone voice rumbled: "*Head for the roundhouse, Nellie, they'll never corner you there."* Suddenly he stopped. He was still having trouble with those left-hand leaps. He needed piano lessons. Where in the hell was Jason Angeletti?

Jason wondered why Gordon Throckrush always chose unlikely places to meet. In this all-night diner, Jason couldn't tell the truck drivers from the waitresses. Gordon sat at a booth in the back, seemingly oblivious to his surroundings, including the people that were staring at him.

"Hey man," he said. "You got a lot on your mind."

"Gordon, this thing is getting serious."

"You mean the spook thing?"

"Remember the guy I told you about, Harry Cone? Well, he's powerful."

"Sure! He's the big spook."

"Don't you see, Gordon? He wants me there."

"So?"

"I might be able to do something."

"Like what?"

"Something in music. I couldn't just sit in a cubicle and shuffle paper. Maybe I'll create some kind of program that

sends artists around the world with a big competition and—"
He looked up.

Gordon was intensely focused on his meat loaf. The gravy ran
down both corners of his mouth.

"Gordon, this could be big!" Jason began making notes on a
napkin. "I'm going to write this up and send it to Harry
Cone. Maybe it'll give some focus to this job thing. What
should I call it? 'The Musical Emissary Program' or 'The
Musical…'"

"How about 'The Spooks Are Coming Program.'"

Jason looked at Gordon's lemon meringue pie and thought the
meringue was indistinguishable from Gordon's hair.

"You sent me a what? What do you mean a proposal?"

"Didn't you get it?" Jason was incredulous. "A job proposal to
create a music program. I mailed it over a week ago."

Harry had not gotten it, and figured instantly that it had been
intercepted. When he heard the word "music," he looked at his
executive assistant, the blond man with the scar. "Get me that
proposal and then fix Angeletti's hiring, or I'll make your ass
grass from here to Kokomo."

Jason could feel the wrath over the telephone lines.

"Meanwhile, Jason, I want you to call me back collect if you don't hear from somebody by close of business today."

"But the government won't accept collect calls."

"Who said that?" Harry practically shouted into the speakerphone. Then he calmed down and started speaking in measured tones. The contrast was startling. "Jason, I guarantee you will hear from someone this afternoon who cares very much about their job. And during that time, there will be some casualties up here in this war of wills." The last word was faint as though he was walking away. Then the line disconnected.

At exactly 5:30 p.m., another secretary introduced a Mr. Nate Hinchmin over the phone.

"I'm associate director of administration and personnel, and I'm sending you some forms. Please fill them out and enclose a list of every address at which you've lived during the past twenty years."

"What's that for, Mr. Hinchmin?"

"FBI check. Then we'll have to get White House clearance. Do you know anybody who can vouch for your political credentials in the party? We would prefer not to use the director for that."

"Well, my father belongs, I think."

"That's all right, then. Maybe we can use the senator from his home state."

"Mr. Hinchmin, what ever happened to Ed Stanley?"

"He's being sent to the island of Wawatootsie, off the Ivory Coast."

"Why?"

"The director wants him out of Washington. He didn't process your hiring quickly enough."

"And Rollie Lovemore?"

"He's still here, but you won't be in his bureau."

"Based on my experience so far, you're going to have your work cut out for you."

"That doesn't bother me, Mr. Angeletti. I've solved bigger stuff as an assistant to two National Security Advisors. You see, I'm originally from the State Department."

"Then I should tell you that I'm beginning to have reservations about this whole thing, and perhaps I should just pass on it."

There was a silence for about six seconds, and then a soft intake of air that repeated itself. Mr. Hinchmin was panting.

"You can't do that, not at this point. You'll have to reconsider. The director wants this, and there's too much at stake."

"What's at stake?"

Another pause.

"The agency, sir. We understand that you will be an asset."

"Mr. Hinchmin, you are indeed a diplomat. What is the target date for this asset?"

"The first day of next month."

"That's next week," Jason said with surprise.

"Indeed, and you are being brought in as a political appointee."

CHAPTER TWO

*T*he drive into Washington took several hours from East Chalmers. It was taken up with thoughts of just having closed his apartment and the logistics of moving into the new place he was renting in the Capitol Hill district of D.C. The agency had sent a check for relocation expenses, and it was more money than Jason had ever had in his life. He used part of it to buy clothes: some suits—pinstripe as per the Washington uniform of the day—shirts, and shoes. Then he had his old, beat-up Dodge tuned up. Now he was thinking about the "leave of absence" he had signed that morning at the university. He turned on the radio. He was close enough to Washington to get the classical music station, and this small pleasure sent his thoughts on yet another path. By the time he got to the Baltimore-Washington Parkway, it dawned on him that this was a milestone in his life. He might even get to meet

Marilyn Goodrump. He imagined what she looked like—high cheekbones certainly. Then the Washington Monument came into view, and he felt another surge of excitement. He would be a part of it all. Not for long, of course, because it was a digression. He was, after all, an artist, but it would be a respectable hiatus.

He turned onto Independence Avenue and into the underground parking beneath the building. Uniformed men approached, and he gave them the special card he had been sent after his FBI clearance went through. Then he took the elevator to the main lobby. Suits and briefcases were everywhere, and people rushing around with ID cards dangling from their necks. Security police guarded the elevators. They sat at desk in front of a metal detector which in turn was in front of a huge American flag. They already had his name.

"Mr. Angeletti. You report to the Security Intelligence Secretariat for vetting and secured de-briefings."

"I beg your pardon?"

"You're gonna have your picture taken. Go to the eighth floor."

He rode the elevator up, thinking this was already different from anything at summer music camp.

"You gotta sit still for this picture," said the agency photographer. "It's the identification photo."

Jason looked at the camera and was beginning to feel a sense of purpose. Even though he hadn't voted in the last election, he felt a surge of patriotism. Sounding in his imagination were the strains of the heroic opening movement of the *Eroica* Symphony of Beethoven: Napoleon leading his troops into battle or crowning himself emperor at Notre Dame. Jason thrust his chin out and tried to look severe, like the figure in a picture he had once seen, General MacArthur landing in the Philippines. "How do I look?" he said.

"Like a CIA spook," came the reply.

A shudder went through him. He hadn't heard the word "spook" since Gordon Throckrush used it.

The photographer was curious. "How high up are you, anyway?"

"Sorry?"

"I haven't seen you before. Are you a big shot or a dwarf?"

"I'm afraid I—"

"Everybody's gotta be somethin' or they ain't nothin'. What's your GS level, man?"

"I'm not sure. Mr. Hinchmin said we'd worry about that later."

"Hinchmin! He's big. He's one of them presidential guys."

"What do you mean?"

"He's got to be—whattya call it?—confirmed by the Senate.

He's gotta have big-time friends to get that job. He ain't never been down here with us stiffs."

"I don't know Hinchmin that well." Jason was trying to assuage the man. "I was brought in by Harry Cone."

The photographer froze. His wide-eyed stare burned into Jason's skull. "Then you're bigger than Hinchmin! You got the big tuna behind you." He surveyed Jason up and down as though making a purchase. "But they're already sayin' Cone's nuts. That makes no difference to me though. I ain't one of them political appointees who has to kiss his butt. I'm here for life."

Jason was given a large desk in the Office of Performing and Visual Arts. Stacks of briefing papers and books about the agency were placed at his disposal by people who could not answer his questions as to what was in them.

The director of the office, a Foreign Service Officer, was a tall, mannish woman of indeterminate age. Jason figured she could not have reached her reverence for procedure in anything less than forty years. She was not amused by Jason's presence nor, for that matter, by anything.

In fact, no one seemed particularly pleased he was there. A certain fake courtesy permeated everything, and he was given nothing to do. He decided that he would not languish in this state of limbo. He would write a memorandum about his music program and send it to Harry. That should get things moving.

He called the office director on the phone. "Who should I ask to type something for me?"

"Why don't you come into my office, and we'll discuss it."

As he walked in, Bonita Baracuddle looked at him with no expression.

Jason felt a chill.

"What is it exactly that you wish to have typed?"

"A memo," he said.

Suddenly, there was a flicker of life force in the woman. Blood began circulating behind her pancake makeup.

"What memo?" she asked.

"I've written a memo to the director about my proposed music program."

"That would have to go through me as director of this office. All memos from the Office of Performing and Visual Arts go through me."

"What do you mean, 'through you'?" Jason imagined ghosts going through doors.

Bonita drew herself up in the chair, so that she loomed even larger. "Every memo that comes out of this office has my signature on it, or my approval if you wish."

"But Harry Cone's a friend of mine. Why do I have to make this memo so official, so damn public? It's just like a letter to someone I know."

"Procedure." Bonita said every syllable slowly and reverently. Then she pursed her lips as though the word gave some sensate pleasure.

Jason went back to his office and called Harry. It was much simpler.

"The director says to come up right now," his secretary said.

Jason moved quickly down the corridor toward the elevator and waited in the anteroom of Harry's large suite of offices on the eighth floor. Jason had never been there before. It was a starburst of activity. Five special assistants and an executive assistant all huddled in small offices on the outer periphery of a large, secretarial pool. There were computers, teletypes, and fax and copy machines all whirring and sputtering, and people crisscrossing the office carrying pieces of paper. It was frenetic and tense. Finally, a secretary nodded at him. It was time to go in. Jason felt a little queasy as he walked through the door of Cone's personal office. Harry was seated on a chair in the center of an enormous room, wearing a blue suit and red vest. Jason knew red was a power color in Washington. On either side of him were men with notepads. The large window behind the director offered a sweeping view of Pennsylvania

Avenue, and the entire wall next to it was covered with a map of the world, spotted with small, flickering lights to indicate each of the American embassies and consulates. A large desk in the corner somehow looked unimposing against the backdrop, but the colored phones sitting on it were disconcerting. One was red and another blue, and the last was black with a speaker box.

"Welcome to the swamp on the Potomac, Jason." Harry liked his remark and savored it for a moment. The two aids had already begun to write when he cocked his head toward one of them. "I believe you know Mr. Hinchmin, on my right."

A slightly built man with a receding hairline and thick glasses looked up.

"And this is my executive assistant, Bill Barron, on my left."

The younger man with blond hair and a scar stopped writing. "My wife and I went canoeing once around East Chalmers," he said. "It's a neat place."

Jason let the remark hang out to dry and turned back toward Harry. He didn't know what the protocol was. Thankfully, Harry seized the initiative.

"Jason has come up with an idea which will help American musicians." Harry turned his head slightly toward Bill Barron without looking at him. He spoke each word slowly with his teeth clenched. "It's a very good idea that will save the taxpayers a lot of money."

The two men started writing furiously. Jason could hear the scratching on their notepads.

"And because Jason Angeletti is a valuable asset, we are going to make him a star in every corner of the world."

Suddenly, the scratching stopped, and both men looked up.

"I want him to do a thirty-minute film on how to play the piano, and we'll distribute it overseas. Put in all the things that helped me so much in those lessons, Jason. We'll use double imagery, and the embassies will take the finished product to local conservatories and classrooms. We'll translate it into Spanish, French, and Arabic, whatever. Then, by the time we send you over there, you'll be a household name. Just take a look at that map, Jason. You'll be able to go anywhere in the world!"

Jason looked at the flickering lights on the wall and felt like the guest on a game show.

"What do you think?" asked Harry.

"I don't think it's possible to learn how to play the piano from a thirty-minute film. I really came up here to…"

Harry's eyes flashed. "I am sure you will do an excellent job."

By this time, the director was in front of his speakerphone, trying to get the head of the agency's TV studios on the line.

"This is Harry Cone," he barked, "and I want to share some thoughts. In my travels throughout the world, I have noticed that piano playing in places like fifty miles outside of Vienna, is in decline. In accordance with our mission to teach people about American culture, I have asked Jason Angeletti to do a film about how to play the piano in hopes of upgrading virtuosity around the globe. Please make all the necessary arrangements."

The silence was uncomfortably long. Finally, the disembodied voice in the box cleared its throat and said, "Yes, sir."

Harry turned off the speakerphone. "Not bad, huh?" He was proud of his performance, and his head bobbed a little. Then it stopped as a thought crossed his mind. "And speaking of upgrading piano playing, I need a little help myself. Got any tips?"

Jason thought quickly, and then as they walked to the door, tried to explain a particular finger stroke. When he put his hand on Harry's arm to demonstrate, the men who had been seated on the couch jumped as though a shot had been fired. They soon settled back; there would be no assassination attempt after all. Jason got in the elevator and pressed the button for the second floor—the arts office. He felt he was going from one fantasy world to another.

The television studios were located in a separate building, and it took a twenty-minute ride in a government shuttle to transport people there. Jason liked the atmosphere at the studios better than at the main agency, and didn't mind being put there on detail for one month to make Harry's film. The employees were more cheerful and even displayed pictures of Harry Cone on the walls of the bunker—like corridors. *That was something you would never see at the main building*, he thought. But the employees at the TV studio were thriving under Harry's tenure. Cone had revitalized the entire section with projects which involved the agency's transmitting, via satellite, a variety of information hookups.

Jason had a good time wandering around the building. It didn't feel like the government. And when they put makeup on him for the screen tests, he almost felt like a star. It was a big deal, too, when they repainted the main studio for his video and brought in graphic artists and suggested camera angles. But he knew he would eventually have to produce something. The script would have to be good; he was working on that. They gave him an office in which to write and put the library at his disposal. If he had any questions, he was told to ask the librarian, Merlina Oyassis. She was an important resource in the TV studios, so he decided to find her.

He wound his way along the passageways. It was an older building with few windows, and most of the offices were below street level. Everything was lit with elongated fluorescent tubes attached to a drop ceiling, which provided a constant buzzing glare and surreal hue. He followed all the directions until he came to a water cooler, where he abruptly turned left. Suddenly, he was inside a small cubicle and head-to-head with the cover of a magazine tabloid. Merlina Oyassis was holding it in front of her face. In front of her desk was a thirty-five-inch color television on a portable stand. It was tuned to a soap opera that played softly in the background, and behind her swivel chair was a man giving Merlina a back massage. Jason recognized him as a cameraman.

"Hi, I'm Jason Angeletti."

Merlina slowly lowered the magazine and looked him over. "Oh, you're Coney-poo's piano teacher." Her classically beautiful face and olive complexion belied her thirty years in government service.

"How did you know?"

"Somebody leaked it out of the front office. It's all over the agency."

"Why is everybody so interested?"

"Because it's not boring. We had a tuba player here. He worked in the New Hampshire primary or something, but they got rid of him because he couldn't do anything. Hell, nobody wanted tuba lessons. You're different though. You give piano lessons to the big kahuna himself. That's access, man!"

"I haven't given him any lessons recently."

"You mean Coney-poo is without his piano lessons now? Well, that's all right. He can just watch your film. That's probably why we're doing it anyway."

"You sound like you know him."

"Are you kidding? He's crazy about me. Whenever he comes to this building, the jackals upstairs trot me out because they know he likes me. I take his coat and talk real jazzy to him. He loves it. Lately, he's been coming into my office just to visit, and he's even fired some people over my phone. I consider that an act of intimacy that he chose to share with just me."

Jason tried to get away from the piano-teacher thing. "I really came here to start a music program." He felt better saying it.

Merlina was beginning to sense an end to her boredom and this man needed protection. "Listen, honey, people don't start new things in the government. And besides, a lot of people don't like Coney-poo, which means they won't like you. So it'll be next to impossible to start anything anyway. Why don't you just keep out of sight and take your check to the bank like the other schlemiels?"

"You don't sound as if you like political appointees."

"I don't dislike them; I feel sorry for them. When they come in, they're all on fire. But when they leave, they look like soot, and you have to sweep them out. And then, the poor babies take so long to learn the ropes that by the time they do, it's *adiós*."

"I need some information, Merlina. It's for a big close on the film, a real smash ending."

"Do you mean the thing you called about the other day? You want to know where this guy's heart is buried, right?"

"Yes, Chopin, the great Polish composer. They buried him in Paris but took his heart out and buried it somewhere else. I've got to find out where. It fits in with my big finish."

"I tried, honey. I really did. There's nothing in this library, and the closest thing they've got at the main building is a biography of John Philip Sousa."

"What about the Library of Congress?"

"They sent over two books on open-heart surgery. I think there was some miscommunication."

"You mean there's nothing in the whole government that—"

"I just don't think the government is set up for this kind of thing, snookums. It's too funky. But if you need something quick, there just might be somebody around here who can run with it. C'mon, let's go see him."

They went downstairs to the offices below street level. The corridors were damp and painted in neuter beige. The lighting was dim and flickering, and a persistent electric buzz resonated in the air. The smell of exhaust fumes rose from traffic passing by some of the open windows. It was dingy and dank, and Jason wondered who they would put down there.

"What's this person's name, Merlina?"

"Richard Boardman."

"What's he doing down here?"

"They don't know where else to put him."

"What do you mean?"

"Well, Richard is a Foreign Service Officer who opted out. He couldn't take the system. He's gifted. He graduated from Brown, and he speaks fluent French. I think he got a five on the Foreign Service exam—that's the highest. Then things went bad. He married a local in Mogadishu, and when they came back here, she split with her green card. He went to a psychiatrist, and when the Foreign Service review board found out, they refused to promote him. Now, he's trying to get out on disability."

"What's his disability?"

"He's always drunk."

They passed the video library and turned a corner toward the water cooler. Suddenly, Merlina ducked through a door into an area where several small offices branched off from an open space. Other than traffic noises in the distance, there was a dead stillness. All the cubicles were empty, save one in the rear corner. There sat a man with a much younger and softer face than his cropped, white hair suggested. There was nothing on his desk: no "in" or "out" boxes, no files or anything on the pale walls, not even a window. It was a tiny room, entirely bare, save for the desk, the telephone, and the one solitary human being.

"Richard, this is Jason Angeletti."

Richard Boardman could not focus well nor hold his head steady, but he spoke instantly. "I know you. You're Harry Cone's piano teacher. Can you get me out of here?"

"Why don't you ask someone more important than me?"

"Like who?"

Jason had to think. His mind went back to all the calls he had received in East Chalmers. He grabbed a name. "Rollie Love-more, for example."

"I know him. We've discussed bowel movements. He has the same parasite I do, except he got his in Mexico, and I got mine in Haiti."

Merlina needed to get things back on track. Chopin's heart would be more fun. "Richard, we want to know where Chopin's heart is."

Richard Boardman looked ponderously at one, then the other. "How in the hell do I know? I can't even find this place. Somebody drives me."

Merlina pleaded. "But, Richard, you've got contacts. You could find out."

"Oh, for Christ's sake!" His head fell back uncontrollably. It stayed there while he pretended to look at the ceiling. Then he grabbed both arms of his swivel chair for support and tried to propel his body forward into an upright posture.

"Maybe Olga might know."

"Who's Olga?" Jason and Merlina spoke almost simultaneously.

"Princess Olga LaTushka. She's a Polish neighbor of mine. She's also a lesbian. Would that bother you?"

"Let's try it," Jason said.

Richard dialed the number with an extended little finger. "Olga, this is Richard Boardman. I need to know where Chopin's heart is located as soon as possible, okay? Try to get back to me before close of business. Call me on my private line though; otherwise, they won't put you through."

When he put the phone down, it missed its cradle and there was a beeping sound. Oblivious, Richard turned toward Jason.

"That was her answering machine. If she doesn't call back, she's a prick." His head fell backward again but still remained in its socket. He stared at the ceiling as though ruminating. "She's probably a prick anyway."

Jason was embarrassed and got up to leave.

"Wait a minute, Angeletti! You gotta get me outta here! Let's plan this thing. When's the next time you're gonna give Harry Cone a piano lesson?"

"I haven't given him any lessons, Richard."

"Just my luck. A hot dog! You're doing all this for your country, right?"

On their walk back, Jason was quiet. "Why do they keep him around… and in a place like that?"

Merlina shrugged. "Because it's practically impossible to fire a career employee, and they don't want anybody to see him."

Chinatown felt like just the right place to be. It was dingy, and you could get lost in one of the little holes that boasted chow fun or crabs in black bean sauce. The booths were not comfortable, but the trade-off was anonymity, and that is what Jason Angeletti needed this night. He had a lot to sort out. Harry Cone's film was completed, and Jason had just seen the first screening. He had given it his all. He had even found where Chopin's heart was buried—in a cathedral in Warsaw—and used that in his "big finish." But it was all clear to him now. The film was god-awful, a big flop.

Merlina told him the TV studio had offered it via diplomatic pouch to all of the two hundred ninety four American embassies and consulates around the world, but not one had responded. The only request was from Harry Cone who wanted it sent to his home in Rock Creek Park through the agency's "routing and transmittal" service. After two Brandy Collinses he settled into that pleasurable booze haze which makes confrontation with oneself more genial. He eyed the waitress, whose English he couldn't understand, and wondered if she could learn to play the piano when that damn film was translated into Chinese. His self-criticism was turning into self —flagellation, so he ordered another drink. This film was the stupidest thing he had ever done. He had prostituted himself, and it cost the taxpayers plenty. Maybe it was a mistake to come into the government.

He toyed with his egg foo young. It was a generic dish, and he wondered if it was really Chinese. He yearned for something authentic in life.

His booth was next to the entrance which faced the main thoroughfare of a bad area in town. He had just finished his third Brandy Collins when a street person walked in unannounced and sat in his booth directly opposite him.

He looked at Jason, saying nothing, then down at the food on the table. Owing to the man's large size, the management pretended not to notice.

Jason simply accepted his presence; he would accept things more readily now. Maybe it was shell shock from having been in the government for the last six weeks, or maybe it was the brandy. Anyway, this intrusion was blending into a continuum of surrealism.

The waitress stood in a corner, watching with the studied detachment of someone leafing through mug shots at the local police station. She saw Jason sip his drink as the vagrant started eating Jason's meal with his fingers. Any conversation between the two men was impossible because the consumption of food occurred at a frenzied pace.

The street person picked apart the dish with fingers that protruded through worn, cloth gloves. They were discolored fingers, the fingers of frostbite and rummaging. Gravy dripped from them, but so did avarice and hunger. The man needed more.

Under his pleasure dome, Jason had the clarity of thought to order steamed dumplings, which would allow the man to take individual pieces without contaminating the surrounding fare. Jason wondered if his quick thinking had developed from his new bureaucratic trade. If so, it was worth celebrating with another drink.

The steamed dumplings came quickly, but Jason's ruminations were deep and distracted him from his own hunger. He sat nursing his drink while his mind replayed the events of the last six weeks. There would be no more films about how to play the piano. He would make a mark for himself through his music program-the Musical Emissary Program. He had to get back to the main agency and get that project moving. He thought of Bonita Baracuddle and winced. She had been out of his mind for a while. But Harry could help; this time he would ask him directly. Jason brightened. Now he was hungry.

He looked at the plate of steamed dumplings, but there were none left. The street person belched and licked his fingers. It took Jason three tries to get up and out of the booth. He didn't know things had become that unmanageable, that four drinks had taken such a toll. He asked the waitress for a cab, but she had already called one. On his way out, he ordered sweet and sour pork for the street person. *I can afford it*, he thought. The government had paid him well to make Harry's film.

The lobby of the main agency had the same ordered coldness as a corporate lobby. There were artificial potted trees, multiple sets of elevators, and the hushed hustle of people who looked past each other on their way to another hour of the day. It was not like the classic government buildings on Constitution or Pennsylvania Avenues. This was a modern building with a fast-food restaurant and deli just off the foyer and a hotel in the back. It was cheaply built in order to get the building appropriations approved by Congress, and it suffered from eight floors of dropped ceilings and poor ventilation. Employees there, who were familiar with the small spaces and compressed humanity, did not trust decisions made in the building after 4:00 p.m. since, by then, oxygen was at a minimum. It was not a pleasant place to be, and Jason was not pleased at being back.

As he walked the bland corridors of the fifth floor, he felt like the enemy. He had been gone a month doing the film, and now that he was back, he had that down feeling of being an outsider in unfriendly territory. He rounded the corner of the long, narrow hallway leading to the complex of arts offices.

When he got to the secretarial pool, he could see his old office. It was dark but looked inviting. He went in, turned on the light, and shut the door. It was a refuge but not a good enough one. He turned the lock on his door—his office was one of the few that had a lock—and he felt better. *It was getting serious*, he thought. No, not serious, ridiculous. He had to get that music program going immediately. He sat at his desk for the rest of the day and read some of the manuals of operation and briefing books that littered the room. He intended to learn about the agency. Early that evening, he drafted a memo:

Memorandum to: Bonita Baracuddle AO/F

From: Jason Angeletti AO/F

Emphasis should now be given toward the mechanics of putting into place a selection process in the fifty states in order to find classical music artists of the highest level. These artists should not be well known nor under professional management but deserving of both. Their purpose will be to serve as musical emissaries overseas for the United States government through concert performances and other corollary activities associated with classical music and diplomacy. We should start with pianists.
(1) Clearances should be obtained through the General Counsel, Mr.George Ogerthorpe, regarding

the question of: Under what domestic authority can the agency engage in such an enterprise?

(2) Given the ICCA's present interdependence with other agencies for the selection of arts programs overseas, it would be helpful to investigate—again through general counsel—the possibility of any loopholes in agreements with these existing agencies which can help pave the way for a more independent ICCA-selection process.

(3) It will be necessary to learn the feasibility of advertising the program broadly through any information service presently within the agency for the purpose of attracting candidates.

The next morning, the sun shone brightly over the city. Employees at the agency began their day by getting coffee at the deli or the fast-food restaurant just off the lobby. Jason spilled coffee on his pant leg as he walked into his office, but he wasn't paying attention. There was a memo from Bonita Baracuddle lying on his desk.

Memorandum to: Jason Angeletti AO/F

From: Bonita Baracuddle AO/F

The musical emissary idea, as you have described it, is

*not feasible during this fiscal year, owing to budgetary
constraints in the Office of Performing and Visual Arts.*

He stood up so abruptly that the swivel chair shot backward. The memo was outrageous. The new fiscal year was
only just beginning. That meant he would have nothing to do
for the next twelve months.

"We'll find something for you to do, Jason. Don't worry."
Bonita Baracuddle was not fazed that he had marched into her
office. She had expected it.

"But I want to do this—the Musical Emissary Program. That's
why I came."

"You are a staff specialist. That's what your job description
states. That means your duties are broad enough that you may
be asked to do other things." Bonita smiled slightly, as a
hunter might in observing trapped prey. "But frankly, there is
another more immediate problem." She savored the moment
by pushing an object on her desk to another spot. "You owe a
payback on your voucher."

"What do you mean?" Jason was now as alert as he had ever
been in his life.

"When you came into the agency, you were given certain
moneys as part of a reimbursement for your relocation
expenses. But apparently, you haven't produced any receipts."

"I wasn't told to keep my receipts. In fact, I tried to give some of that money back after the trip when I found I hadn't spent it all. But one of your program officers, the one who briefed me on the voucher, told me the government wasn't set up to take money back. It's long gone now."

"We'll require that money, and perhaps other moneys as well. Unless, of course, you have your receipts from that entire period."

"I told you I don't have any receipts. That program officer never told me they were required."

"He says he did."

"Well, then, it's his word against mine."

"Unless you can prove otherwise, I must insist on reclaiming that sum." Bonita assumed a regretful air, but she was not finished. "And finally—"

Jason moved forward to the edge of his chair, so he could more easily lurch at her.

"I must ask you to write down everything you and Director Cone have ever discussed in the privacy of his office when there were no other parties present."

Jason's face was frozen in contempt. "I refuse. Those conversations are entirely private."

"But we need to know what was said so we are not caught unprepared. What if he is planning another one of his, eh, projects? You must realize that you're in the government now; nothing is private."

Jason bolted from the room and down the corridor. He had to get to the street for some air. When he got to the lobby, he burst through the doors to the street outside and walked back and forth in front of the building. He would have to borrow the money to pay it back. And he would have to call Harry. He went right back in and used the phone at the security desk on the main floor. They switched him through to Bill Barron.

"The director's busy right now, Jason. And, under such circumstances, I handle his calls. What's up?"

Jason lowered his voice. "Listen, a lot of things are funny down here."

"You sound like you're in an underground bunker during the London blitz."

"Maybe I am." Jason explained what had happened.

Barron was curt. "You'd better learn to get along with those people. Don't cause the director any problems."

The loud click at the end precipitated another run to the street for air. Jason's mind was reeling; his eyes and ears were assaulted by a jumble of images amid the blaring of traffic. Why was this happening? He walked around the block. No money for the program? He hadn't even started it yet! Did Harry know about this? Or did Harry order it? Why was Jason even there? Should he leave? He wondered if he could ever get through to Harry again after Bill Barron had shut him off like a spigot. And what about the money he had to pay back? Why hadn't somebody told him? Was he being set up? A chill went through his body.

A tall man in his midthirties stood at the street corner wearing a mustache, a trench coat, and a felt hat. "You're Jason Angeletti, aren't you?" The man wore no expression on his face.

"How did you know?"

"Oh, everybody in the agency knows who you are. You gave Harry Cone piano lessons, and you're trying to start a music program."

Jason didn't feel famous, just suspicious—as if he were being watched from every angle.

"I'm Edmund O'Rourke," the man said abruptly. "I'm director of the Office of Personal Exchange here at the agency. How's your program going, anyway?"

Everybody was something, it seemed, director of this or that, or assistant director or assistant to the assistant. "Fine," he heard himself say.

"Well, you don't look fine." It was a personal comment that didn't fit with O'Rourke's deadpan expression and monotone. "C'mon, we're both political appointees, and that means we're brothers."

"That's a pretty big leap of faith to make with a perfect stranger, isn't it, Mr. O'Rourke?"

"The name's Ed, and it's no leap of faith in the trenches. Its political combat—us against the 'lifers.'"

"Who?"

"The career people who can never be fired. You're already defined by being a political appointee; your friends and enemies have been made, and you've got to know who they are."

"Sounds like a gulag."

"Not at all. In fact, it's exciting if you've been trained for it."

"How do you train for it?"

"Plenty of ways—think tanks, youth movements, writing articles, state conventions…"

"Well, I've never done any of that, so I must be in the wrong business."

"All the more reason to trust someone."

Jason decided to go for broke. "Okay, things are terrible. I just called Bill Barron, and—"

"What are you doing dealing with Barron? He's career!"

Jason stared blankly.

"We're the people brought in to carry out the president's goals,

Jason. That's what I've been trying to tell you. We're political appointees, and the career people aren't too keen on us. They think our jobs take important jobs away from them, and they're right. But if they were in charge, nothing the president wanted would ever get done—unless, of course, they agreed to it. Don't you see? If it weren't for us, they'd be in charge."

The traffic light changed, and people were looking at both of them while they crossed the street. O'Rourke changed the subject and said something else that did not fit with his poker face. "Did you know that I love music? I was in the arts once; I tried to be an actor. Why don't you come over for dinner tonight? We'll talk some more."

Ed's house was in a two-story, narrow, dark-brick townhouse typical of Southeast, Washington, D.C. It was on Pennsylvania Avenue just east of the Capitol, in the vortex of power, history, and physical unsafety.

O'Rourke greeted him with the same emotional impassivity as that afternoon, except with a booming voice. Music was playing loudly through the stereo speakers—Beethoven's great Ninth Symphony. The living room was dimly lit, featuring furniture that didn't match, and an orange, kind of Rembrandt hue emanated from the light under an old tasseled lampshade. A suit of armor stood in the corner, along with samurai swords over the fireplace, hundreds of books against the wall, and a gun case that was locked. O'Rourke turned the music down and offered him a glass of French Cabernet.

Jason carried it to the immense bookcases. The books were all hard cover, mostly about political thought, philosophy, and history. He started to feel the warm glow of the wine as the music on the turntable moved into the great chorale movement of Beethoven's Ninth Symphony.

"Freude, freude," cried the basso. "Joy, joy!"

Jason sank into the sofa. The recitative in the bass introduced a full chorus against the forces of the instrumental players. An army of full orchestra, full chorus, and four soloists burst forth so powerfully that Jason had to get up and walk around. The sound almost drowned out the doorbell. O'Rourke came racing in from the kitchen to turn the music down and open the door.

"Jason, I'd like you to meet our other guest for this evening… Marilyn Goodrump."

Jason wheeled around.

Marilyn entered the room diffidently, with the feline instinct of knowing where everything was and while yet remaining detached from it. "Mr. Angeletti," she said in a whisper.

The sopranos in the background sang softly the words of the poet Schiller: *"Joy, beautiful spark of gods, Daughter of Elysium, We enter drunk with fire."*

Marilyn glided across the floor as if on a cloud, her hourglass figure keeping pace with some mute melody. "I thought we'd meet one day." She came closer, wearing a half smile. Her arm was extended. Jason tried not to look at her cleavage, which he had already determined looked like a canyon in the Pyrenees. He raised himself up to his full height, his muscles taught. "You... You can call me Jason," he said, shaking her hand.

The stereo speakers swelled with the choir and full orchestra, breaking into the mighty chorus from the "Ode to Joy."

O'Rourke set the dinner table with a candle, and the flickering light cast huge shadows against the wall. In the murkiness, Jason thought even that suit of armor in the corner might come to life. As dinner was about to begin, the host changed the music to the Berlioz *Requiem*. Marilyn sat at the center of the table, and O'Rourke and Jason at either end. She whisked her auburn hair back with an attractive, offhand gesture. Jason wondered if she was O'Rourke's girlfriend or if he, himself, might stand a chance.

Suddenly, O'Rourke stood up and the chair screeched against the hardwood floor. He thrust out his glass. "I want to offer a toast to our great president and the new administration in hopes that they get everything they want!"

Marilyn quickly lifted her glass with a nod. Jason lifted his without knowing a single thing the administration wanted.

The entrée came next, an enormous cut of sirloin. Marilyn

seemed too demure for the immodest hunk in front of her but dug in anyway.

"When we last spoke, you were working for Rollie Lovemore."

She nodded at Jason. "Yes, I was his secretary."

"Was?"

"Now I'm Ed's deputy." She turned toward O'Rourke and smiled.

"Wow. That was fast."

"Oh, it's already been a couple months, and in Washington, that's a lifetime."

"What are your responsibilities?"

"I help give grants of up to sixteen million dollars to the private sector."

Jason glanced at O'Rourke who looked impassive and twirled his mustache.

Another bottle of wine was opened, a milder Beaujolais, and Ed lit a cigar. "My house is a free zone for those who like Havanas." He blew an enormous ring of smoke into the shadows.

"Too bad Marvin isn't here," said Marilyn. "He likes cigars, too."

"A great man," said O'Rourke.

"Who?"

"Marvin Mariah. You would have liked him, Jason."

"I spoke with him once."

"Right," O'Rourke continued. "That's before Harry fired him for requisitioning a shoulder holster…"

"I heard about that."

Marilyn set her napkin down. "I met him at a picnic sponsored by the party, and he thought I had potential. He brought me into the government and even got me White House clearance…"

"What were you doing at the time?" Jason asked.

"I was a waitress at Charlie's restaurant in Tysons Corner." Marilyn crinkled her nose coquettishly and took a sip of wine. She looked at Jason with a naughty smile.

He thought she might have winked at him but wasn't sure. The wine was working on everyone. Marilyn got up a little unsteadily, and offered to bring out the dessert.

Jason's eyes followed her into the kitchen. He thought it paradoxical that such a seemingly shy woman would wear a skirt so tight you could see her appendectomy scar.

Three dishes of vanilla ice cream were placed on the table, each with a cinnamon stick in the center. But everyone reached for the wine. Suddenly, O'Rourke turned toward Jason looking like a man who had witnessed a dastardly act. "The guerilla bureaucrats are after you, Jason... in order to embarrass the president."

Jason's eyes widened. "But I don't even know the president." He kept to himself that he had never known anyone who had been president of anything.

The "Tuba Mirum" from the *Requiem* began drifting through the speakers.

"You see, Jason, in the political world, you spring forth from Harry as a child comes from its mother's womb. He is your godfather, and if his head falls, the rest of the body follows. Here's the way the bureaucrats see it, like a chain: you, then Harry Cone, then the president."

A trumpet called the dead to judgment, bringing four brass bands crashing antiphonally into a fortissimo: *Day of wrath! O day of mourning! See fulfilled the prophets' warning...*

Jason looked down at the melting ice cream. O'Rourke kept pressing.

"That's why you should come to my shop. You'll have every-thing you want or need, and you'll be protected. Set up an appointment with Harry for the two of us, and we'll make our case."

Marilyn delivered the *coup de grâce*. "Then I'd be able to help you with your program, Jason."

The next afternoon, he and O'Rourke sat in the waiting room just outside Harry's office. O'Rourke was stiff and military in his bearing, and carried a notepad. There was tense expectancy as everyone waited for Harry to come back from lunch. Finally, he breezed through the glass doors accompanied by a squat, balding man who was about the same age.

O'Rourke sat bolt upright. "That's Robespere."

"Who's Robespere?"

"Harry's deputy, the deputy director of the ICCA—the number two man." There was incredulity in O'Rourke's voice. He figured Jason would have known.

But Mel Robespere did not have a particularly distinguished bearing. He was short, bald, flat-footed, and his eyes danced frenetically. They glanced off of objects and people in the room like darting fish. His real name was Melvin Rabinovitz, but his father had changed it to make it sound a little French.

There was a brief introduction, but Mel looked past the other two men. "Harry, I gotta go. I'm going to negotiate with the Japanese this afternoon, and that takes energy. Everything's the bottom line with them, you know?"

He turned and went through a door that connected the offices of the director and deputy director. Harry followed. Soon, there was laughter coming from behind the door as the two men jousted with Mel's tape recorder.

O'Rourke leaned toward Jason to whisper something, and

Jason strained to listen. The two men's heads were almost touching. "It's like a Marx Brothers movie, isn't it?" O'Rourke's face registered no mirth.

Jason thought the meeting would be an interesting match since there was a dismissive and peremptory aspect to O'Rourke's personality. But as soon as the director walked back into the room, O'Rourke became a submissive foot soldier. The air was chilly. O'Rourke began timorously with a simple "sir?" but Harry cut him off.

"Did I call this meeting or did you? I can't keep things straight right now. There's too damn much going on up here." He grabbed a fistful of crinkly carbon copies—five sheets of appointments for each work day of the week—and threw them in the wastebasket. The gesture looked churlish and sloven-ly. "That takes care of that. I won't need them since this week is gone. It's the end of the week, right?" Harry looked at the two of them abruptly with a decisive, authoritarian glare that demanded an answer.

"Yes, it's Friday," said Jason.

"No, it's Thursday." O'Rourke looked straight ahead.

Harry looked at both of them. "You probably don't even know what year it is. Well, I'm declaring it to be Friday because I want it to be Friday." Harry's head swiveled from side to side like a marionette. He grinned widely, with teeth that gleamed like ivory piano keys.

"I did," said Jason, suddenly.

"You did what?"

"Asked for this meeting."

"What for?"

O'Rourke began writing furiously on his notepad.

"I'd like to move to Ed's shop. It's no good where I am now." Jason was prepared to elaborate, but Harry intervened.

"All right, what else?"

Jason was stunned by the simplicity of what the director had just said. He decided to go for broke. "I need some help, too, for this whole thing to work. It's got to be done right."

O'Rourke chimed in. "As you know, sir, Jason has the idea to hold live auditions in the fifty states to find artists that the agency can send overseas for performances. Great for public diplomacy! But we need to know if it's within the legal purview of the agency."

Harry stood up briskly and walked over to his intercom.

"Get George Ogerthorpe, the general counsel, up here, *pronto!*"

George came into Harry's office perspiring with his coat unbuttoned, draping his massive weight. Suspenders were visible, bulging over piles of flesh. He moved slowly, like some floating oil tanker trying to remain steady, while he reached

for objects to help him in that endeavor. Years of cunning arti-
fice had given him the confidence that he could mask his
drinking problem. So he moved his hand along the entire rim
of the couch until he strategically placed himself next to a
cabinet he could lean against. His yellowish eyes were backdrop to an unhealthy pallor. He turned his pug face toward the
director.

Harry got right to the point. "Can we have live music auditions throughout the fifty states on public money?"

George stolidly raised his head with its great bull neck and
replied fairly evenly, "Well, sir, only if it were not advertised
since that would be a violation of the Bull-Quash Act. That act
prohibits us from letting the American people know what we
are doing since our constituency is exclusively foreign." After
an almost inaudible burp, George smiled and inwardly
congratulated himself on his answer.

Harry moved closer to him and spoke in a biting staccato.
"How in the hell are people going to show up for the auditions
if they don't know about them?"

George pondered for a moment. He had eaten Filet of Grouper
Veracruz for lunch with a double-vodka chaser but didn't think
the director could smell any booze. "I would really like to
research this whole thing for a day before I give you a final
answer." George tried to keep from exhaling.

"What do you mean, research it? You're a lawyer, aren't
you? You're general counsel, aren't you? If you don't know

the answers, then I can find you a smaller office, and I know that'll break your heart."

George, who was usually red, turned white. The heat seemed to rise in the room, and beads of perspiration rolled down his jowls.

Harry's voice began rising, and the words came out like bullets. He circled George and shouted, "Can't you people get off your asses and do something for your paycheck besides consume groceries?"

It seemed to George that all the air had been sucked out of the room. The room seemed to move, tilting like a ship that was listing. Objects appeared doubled, and wave of nausea slithered up the trunk of George's body to his pale, pumpkin-like face. Suddenly, the reptilian part of his brain kicked in and reminded him to start breathing again. He exhaled at last with a great gush of air that smelled like a gimlet. The room promptly appeared right-side up, but now everything was blurred. Perhaps he could find a chair to hold onto or sit down in, but he didn't know the physical proximity of anything around him.

At that moment, a secretary said, "Mr. Cone, the White House is on the line. The president would like to speak to you."

George sensed this was his time to escape. He turned toward the sound of the secretary's voice and only then saw a beam of light. With more effort, he managed to see the outline of a water cooler in the distance and started moving toward it. His squint now took in the door to the outside corridor. He moved more quickly through the door and to the elevator, where he stopped, completely out of breath. He pressed the button several times and thought that he really had to do something about the booze. He had to cut down. Maybe he could eliminate the scotch with milk in the morning and just take an earlier lunch. As he got into the elevator and pressed the button for the seventh floor, he thought he might switch to beer at night. The doors closed, and the elevator went down. It seemed to George that he was always going down.

Jason and O'Rourke had not yet been dismissed, so they stood there like two schoolboys listening to Harry's phone conversation with the president.

When it finally ended, Harry looked up, almost forgetting they were there. He blinked with both eyes simultaneously, then looked at Jason. "Go ahead with your music program, kid. Those lawyers couldn't catch a cold with their clothes off."

CHAPTER THREE

$\mathcal{A}$s Jason settled into his new office under the protective umbrella of Edmund O'Rourke, he busily began to build the foundation for his new music program. Supported now by Harry, he operated with almost reckless abandon. He managed to get donated facilities across the country for audition sites, wrote and obtained clearance for brochures for his program, listing the criteria for contestants, and worked in liaison with various other elements of the agency to determine grant procedures, publicity packets and posters. He obtained the historic Library of Congress as a venue for the final round of the competition and visited "desk officers" representing different regions of the world to see where best to send the musicians. Some people were overly friendly, others hostile. But he persevered by employing horse blinders, looking to neither side. In due course, each of the building blocks was challenged, but Jason relished it, seeing himself as David fighting the Philistines.

Marilyn Goodrump organized employees in the office to stuff packets with the nominating materials and a cover letter to send to every graduate music school and music festival in the United States. It was decided to begin the program with pianists and the schools were each allowed up to two nominees for the first round of auditions. That was a cost-effective way to begin with no agency involvement. The second round would be live auditions throughout the country, and a certain number chosen from those would be brought back to Washington for the finals. Everything was ready to go, but before anything could be sent to the schools, he had to make sure he had the money for the auditions. O'Rourke would surely provide that from his office funds. Jason had only to ask.

"I'm so proud of you." Marilyn kissed him on the cheek. People noticed, since any display of emotion or affection was irregular in that atmosphere. But Jason didn't care and liked acting freely in her presence.

He started to enjoy himself, going to lunch with colleagues, talking about what he was doing, and fitting in somehow. He rented a small grand piano for his little apartment, so he could practice in the early evenings. He even wrote East Chalmers University to say that he wasn't coming back after his "leave of absence" was up.

Everything was going well... until with the suddenness of a

cardiac arrest, O'Rourke was in trouble. An article appeared in the *Washington Post*, saying that he was overly partisan and giving government grants only to those who agreed with his political ideology.

Harry Cone ordered an immediate investigation by the Office of the Inspector General. This involved a seizure of files and three days of interrogation. O'Rourke responded that he had acted only in the spirit of the president. When interviewed by the *New York Times*, he decried the entire exercise as "patently political" and added: "Mudslides accumulate filth as they make their way to the bottom." Edmund O'Rourke's days were clearly numbered.

It was 2:30 a.m. when the phone rang. Normally Jason would not answer it out of a deep sleep, but things were crazy and unsettled now. He wondered who it was?

"Jason, can I buy you a drink?" There was a soft giggle.

"Where are you, Marilyn?"

"Around the corner at Bullfeathers."

He dressed quickly and walked the block down First Street SE, amazed the place was still open. He walked into a dimly lit room, soft with amber colors. The bartender was wiping the bar, and the rancid smell of stale beer hung in the air. All chatter and *eros* had ceased as people, already gone, had to face themselves somewhere else in the quietude of the night. Marilyn sat alone at the bar.

"Can't sleep?" he asked.

"Crazy times," she said, shaking her head, then lifting her glass. "Name your poison, Jason."

He ordered a beer and drank it so quickly that Marilyn asked if he'd like another.

"Booze is cheaper at my place."

She raised her eyebrows, then looked down at her glass, trying to decide what she had already decided. When she lifted her head, their eyes locked for a moment. His face creased into a gentle smile that reassured her, and she reached for her purse. He nodded toward the door.

They walked out together into the night air and into each other's orbit. Not a word was exchanged as he put his arm around her, and they walked the city block back to his place. Once in the apartment, he made no pretense to bringing any drinks. Their first kiss was immediately inside the door. The second was more passionate until she pushed him away.

"I can't do this," she said. "I'm already involved with two other men, Ed O'Rourke and Marvin Mariah."

"Three's company," he said softly.

He awoke the next morning and looked at Marilyn, the outline of her body lying in the folds of the sheet. *A Greek goddess*, he thought. *What did I do to deserve this?* He got up quietly, so he wouldn't disturb her, and went into the bathroom to dress. But any movement in the tiny apartment could hardly be concealed or kept quiet.

Marilyn stirred. "Let's go for breakfast, Jason."

It was a bright weekend morning, and traffic was light, so they walked down Independence Avenue passing book stores and small cafés before settling on scrambled eggs at the Hawk 'n' Dove.

As they walked in, Jason thought about how different bars were in the morning sunlight. Waiters carried steaming plates of eggs and bacon amidst energetic chatter, all part of a new and breaking day. That was decidedly more optimistic than the forced *bonhomie* of cigarette smoke and alcohol that would surely begin in the late evening. He thought of the melancholy fog that hung in the stale air of the empty bar the night before. He wanted nothing to do with alienation. There was enough of it in being an artist, in being alone for hours behind a black box every day. He looked at Marilyn sitting across from him and saw completion. His mind started racing. He wanted her in his personal life, he wanted this to be a regular thing. He waited for an opening.

"You are amazing, Jason."

"Really," he said, swelling with manly pride.

"Yes! You're perceived as one of the most powerful men in the agency, and yet you live in that tiny, little place."

His body seemed to shrink. "I'm not powerful. I don't even have a staff."

"You have direct access to Mr. Cone!" Marilyn's tiny voice rose with a sudden urgency that just as quickly subsided. She took a sip of orange juice. "I think I'll have to break it off with Marvin."

That's at least one down, thought Jason. "Why?" he asked, trying to be casual.

"Because he doesn't have any power any more. He's not as much fun to be around."

Jason threw a zinger. "Looks like O'Rourke is on his way out, too."

Marilyn nodded with the innocently regretful look of a little girl who was about to bury her pet goldfish.

O'Rourke was hamstrung, and so was his back, which was most often out. He was director of his office in name only, his authority having been taken away. Meanwhile, the investigation of his office continued with interrogations of his staff, gossip in the corridors, and tenseness in the air. Word was that he would be gone in a week. In the meantime, he came to the office every day in the acceptable management, pinstripe suit.

"How are you holding up?" someone asked.

"Either the bear gets you or you get the bear; but always dress for the hunt."

Meanwhile, Jason was in limbo. He couldn't begin the auditions since O'Rourke, as an office director, could no longer allocate him any money.

It was on the sixth day of O'Rourke's ordeal that Jason and Marilyn were chatting in Jason's office. The two agreed in comparing the protracted battle to the Bataan Death March. Suddenly, O'Rourke walked in and urgently closed the door behind him. Both Marilyn and Jason thought the same thing: Edmund had finally gotten his pink slip.

O'Rourke's face was alert but somber, like a gravedigger watching Picket's Charge. "Mel Robespere has been fired."

A tremor swept through the room.

"My God," said Marilyn, "the deputy director."

"You're kidding? What happened," Jason asked.

O'Rourke spoke softly. "Mel was involved in hiring into the agency half the children of the president's cabinet: the daughter of the secretary of state works here; the secretary of defense's son; the niece of the national security advisor and others. The Senate Committee on Foreign Relations found out about it and requested all their 171 forms and résumés to determine their qualifications. Mel refused to hand them over when Harry was on one of his overseas junkets. Now the *Washington Post* has the story, and it will break in tomorrow morning's edition. They're calling it 'Babygate.'"

"Weren't any of them qualified?" Jason asked.

"Let's put it this way. One of them had been a security guard at a pitch and putt in Sepulveda, California, and now he's running the Russian Research Division; another worked in a kennel adjusting flea collars, and now she's deputy director of the Office of Academic Exchanges."

"When did this happen?" Jason asked.

"This morning."

"Where's Mel now?" Marilyn said.

"Gone. Harry gave him thirty minutes to get out of the agency and then had security padlock his files. And that's not all, folks." O'Rourke now looked directly at Jason. "I got a call not thirty minutes ago saying that someone at an executive committee meeting this afternoon said, 'Jason Angeletti is a liability to the director because he can be tied into the Baby-gate scandal as Harry Cone's former piano teacher.' There's the implicit threat of a leak from your old friends in the arts bureau."

Harry's limousine rounded the Washington Monument and cut through Fourteenth Street to Pennsylvania Avenue. It was the quickest way to the White House. The guard at the gate had been alerted, but Harry rolled down the darkened window to show his face anyway. The car moved slowly through the gate and over the blacktop path like some great yacht until it settled under the North Portico. A marine guard opened the door and Harry ran up the steps. Again the door was opened for him, and he made his way through the mansion toward the West Wing. Finally, he came to the glass frame door with the presidential eagle emblazoned on it. The quickness with which it opened startled the chief of staff. But the president smiled benignly, watching Harry stand there with two marine guards on either side, each over half a foot taller.

"What's the matter, Harry? Am I late for our appointment at the Jockey Club?"

"Can't go there. A man bit a dog, and the place is swarming with reporters."

The president chuckled. The president's chief of staff, a former prosecutor, well groomed with silver hair, did not.

"I had to get rid of my deputy today. I guess he was selling indulgences or something." Harry smiled, showing all his teeth, and shook his head slightly. He had to keep it light; it was a personnel matter. The chief of staff took more of an interest in the remark than the president. "It'll hit the papers tomorrow," he said, "but I don't think they'll sell many because I've got all my clothes on."

The president laughed again as he got up from his desk. He moved across the soft rug, walking over the Great Seal of the United States, and put his arm on the smaller man's shoulder. "Listen, Harry, my wife and I couldn't live in this town without you and Mary Ellen. Don't worry about a thing."

Harry visibly relaxed. "Did I tell ya? I took my wife to a wife-swapping party last night, and they wanted me to throw in some cash."

The president doubled up with laughter and reached for the back of a chair for support. He wheezed. When the air in his lungs was finally replenished, he managed a loud "haw!" It penetrated the walls.

For the ride back, Harry got the driver to remove his dummy keyboard from the trunk of the limousine. He placed it on his lap and moved his fingers over the silent keys. At a stoplight, he reached toward a video screen impaneled into the back of the seat in front of him and pressed a button. Jason Angeletti's film appeared. Harry turned up the volume and fast-forwarded until he found the exercises he wanted. He followed Jason's instructions, holding one finger down and working the next, until he got bored. As the car moved onto Constitution Avenue, his fingers moved into the patterns of the *Fantaisie Impromptu* of Chopin. Just the feeling of contact with the keys seemed to calm him; his heart rate slowed, and his mind emptied. It was the only thing that relaxed him. When the dome of the Capitol came into view at seventeenth and Constitution, Harry was playing the second, or lyrical theme, of the *Fantaisie Impromptu.* This section had been popularized in an American song entitled "I'm Always Chasing Rainbows." Harry's eyes wandered to the feminine ornament on the top of the Capitol dome, the Statue of Freedom, and he thought of Judy Garland. He had once heard her sing the song and wondered whose version was better, Chopin's or Judy Garland's.

Edmund O'Rourke's final whammy came after another series of negative press articles alleging political extremism. Having been on life support for weeks, he had long since packed his office. Jason and Marilyn helped carry boxes down to the car on his day of departure.

Soon after, it was announced that Marilyn Goodrump would be "acting director" until a new office director could be named. Jason wondered if this would affect their relationship. He watched her move through the office, going from one cubicle to the other, overseeing and dispensing advice. Gone was her vulnerability and demure behavior. She had now absorbed the principles and ideology of the administration, evidenced most dramatically by her military walk where the spikes of her high heels dug into the carpet as though hammering a nail into each plank of the party platform.

"Jason, darling, the office can't write a check. There's no money. The program budget is tied up because of Ed and the investigations. In order to keep your program going, why not try getting funding from Rollie Lovemore upstairs?"

Jason flinched. Rollie was head of the whole bureau and third in line of authority before Harry Cone. But political appointees routinely held up two outstretched index fingers in the shape of a cross whenever they passed his office. It was not pleasant to think of having to go in there and ask for money. But at least Marilyn had just called him darling.

Rollie Lovemore sat alone in his office, enjoying a rare moment of serenity. He felt well, and even the secretary remarked about the color in his cheeks. He settled comfortably in his chair, feeling the softness against his backside, then reached for a cigar. Harry Cone was out of town, and the agency was quiet. Through a ring of smoke, Rollie reflected on how he had gotten to where he was. It had been an accident, like so many things in government or politics. How could it be otherwise? He had been an associate professor of political science at Bella Vista College in West Virginia. Now he was head of all academic scholarships and overseas exchange programs for the U.S. government. *If it hadn't been for Marvin getting whacked,* he thought, he would still be a lowly office director. Now he was a presidential appointee and head of the whole damn bureau. Marvin Mariah had been too hot for Harry Cone to handle. Rollie cried when Marvin got fired; it was in public, too. After all, Marvin had brought him into the government, and Rollie knew that, in politics, you dance with the one who brought you. "What's going to happen to me now?" he said.

Marvin had never seen a man in the government cry and took pity on Rollie. He even recommended him to Harry as the new associate director.

Rollie knew what was necessary to govern and survive in the bureaucracy. It helped to have an arsenal of tricks: body language, strong verbs, cunning, and, of course, tears were all part of it. But tears had to be used judiciously.

He remembered when morale was dangerously low at the agency, and the executive leadership in the bureau had taken part in a professional seminar at Appomattox, Virginia. The focus of the seminar was on how to get in touch with your emotions and deal with stress therapeutically. It proved to be cathartic for Rollie's subordinates when they ganged up on him in the group session. He countered with a plea for under-standing. "It's Harry Cone that's the problem," he said. "I don't want to do a lot of these things, but I'm under orders." The tears were understated, which made the impact all the more powerful on this emotionally contained and buttoned-down group. During the ride home, Rollie wiped away his tears, secure in the knowledge that he had won the hearts and minds of everyone there.

Was this not the goal that Machiavelli had suggested? Rollie thought back to his political science lectures at Bella Vista. *God*, he mused, *it's a lot better living it than lecturing about it. I might even survive these four years.* His eyes started moving around, languidly taking everything in. They came to rest on the east wall of his office. *If I knock that out*, he thought, *I can make this room twice as big.*

Olivetta Montgomery stuck her head through the open door. She was Rollie's secretary, a tall African American woman who had that sublime air of indifference. No one knew how many associate directors she had seen come and go. She even addressed him by his first name. "Rollie, Jason Angeletti's out here to see you."

Rollie's mind raced. *Jason Angeletti*, he thought, *another one of Harry Cone's "wacko" friends.* Well, this was as good a time as any other and would save him a call. Rollie thought back several months to when Jason tried to switch bureaus from the arts office in order to work with O'Rourke. Rollie didn't want him in his bureau and held up the paperwork for six weeks.

When Harry found out, he literally stamped his foot and shouted, "Why can't I get a memo from a friend?" He threatened Rollie with termination at the weekly meeting of top agency executives.

But today, Jason walked into Rollie's office with hands in his pockets and an air of amiability. He had never met Rollie face-to-face, and he needed something. He didn't know what to expect.

Rollie seemed to enjoy the moment. "Jason, my boy, have a seat."

Rollie's smile had down-home warmth, so Jason decided on bluntness. "I need some money for my program, Rollie. I don't have a budget, and I'm setting up all these regional auditions around the country. Musicians will be traveling to the sites, and I don't even have money to send judges out there to hear them. It won't take much, and Harry Cone's big on the idea. He's already authorized it." Jason saved the best for last, certain it would clinch the deal. Rollie might even think Harry sent him in there for the money.

Rollie got up and quietly closed the door. He returned to his desk and picked up a letter. "The director asked me to give you this."

It was all done so quickly that Jason took a moment before looking at it. There was more to this than he had first thought. Perhaps it was a commendation from Harry. The director often did this sort of thing with effusive language, in a kind of vulgar, grand, Hollywood style. He began to read:

Dear Mr. Angeletti:

As you know, you were hired to launch the Musical Emissary Program; thanks to you, that has been remarkably well achieved. With that launching, however, and with the budgetary constraints placed upon this agency, we are now forced to merge the successful Musical Emissary Program into the Office of Performing and Visual Arts in the F Bureau under the leadership of its director, Bonita Baracuddle.

Accordingly, this letter is to thank you for a job well done and to inform you that your non-career status appointment will be terminated, effective in two weeks. As noted in your original letter of appointment, those appointed under political status serve at the pleasure of the director.

I wish to thank you personally for the significant contribution you have made during your service with ICCA. Musical emissaries represent an important new initiative which will greatly enhance our cultural programs. Your diligence and creativity in bringing musical emissaries to the point of takeoff does much to ensure its future success. It has been a pleasure to have you in the Bureau of Intercultural Exchange, and I wish you the very best in future endeavors.

Sincerely,
Roland T. Lovemore
Associate Director
Burea of Intercultural Exchange

It was as if someone had beaten on a giant oil drum some-where in his gut. And then a long, terrifying silence followed by rage and fear. He stared at the letter in a stupor, then mumbled something without knowing what. He forced himself to think. *How could this have happened? Who did it and why? What about the musicians? What about the lease on the apart-ment and resigning from his job at East Chalmers?* He finally blurted, "This is outrageous!"

"You're welcome to talk to the director about it, Jason. I'm just the messenger." It was apparent that Rollie considered the meeting over. But for Jason, it seemed everything was over.

He left abruptly; his anger was too deep. He returned to his office and closed the door. He had no feeling as thoughts careened in his head. Who should he tell? What should he do now?

Marilyn walked in and examined his face. She knew some-thing was wrong. It was unusual that a face would reflect that much emotion in this constrained environment, but she imag-ined Jason felt things more intensely because he was a musi-cian. That made him different in her eyes.

He told her everything. She cried and left his office.

Ten minutes later, Edmund O'Rourke telephoned. "Jason, I just heard. This is outrageous, the most unconscionable thing Harry Cone has ever done. I've still got friends in this town, and we're going to have a war council tomorrow night."

The meeting was held in a townhouse in an elegant part of Georgetown. Jason walked down two steps into a living room that reeked of age with low, wood-beam ceilings and antiques. He was greeted by people clomping around on the hardwood floors. They came to him one at time, speaking in low voices as if to a family member at a wake. Chairs were brought in to accommodate them; they were mostly office directors, their hand-picked deputies, and others whom Jason did not recognize. He watched and listened. He was learning the game. These people also "served at the pleasure" of Harry Cone and could easily be fired at any time. And, surviving that, they would be replaced anyway by a succeeding administration. They were a high-wire act with commensurate pressure and uncertainty; itinerants who came and went, with their only compensation being life on the fast track. They were from somewhere and nowhere, from think tanks and faculties, banks and odd jobs. Everyone knew someone who knew the president, and they were all in his service. They believed in the issues, but that became less of an issue as time passed. And as time passed, the ruthlessness of their environment tipped the scales against peace of mind in a quest for political survival.

The host was an even-tempered, balding man with a beard who directed the Overseas Guest Program, one of the most successful and long-standing cultural exchange programs at the agency. He opened the meeting by greeting everyone with a warm smile and then dispatched his deputy to guard the door from the outside. There were several Foreign

Service Officers who lived nearby, he explained. "It's never a good idea to let your enemies know what you're up to." Then, with a change of expression but without looking at Jason, he said, "Now, ladies and gentlemen, how can we put enough pressure on Harry Cone to get Jason Angeletti rehired?"

In rapid-fire order, there came responses.

"I've already leaked it to the two major newspapers in town and some hill staffers." O'Rourke jerked at his mustache while he spoke. "And even if these journalists don't do the story now, they'll nose around and Cone will know that it could blow up at any time."

The director of the Embassy Libraries Program was next. "I've talked to one of the cable networks. They're thinking of doing it as a human-interest story."

Jason felt like a fly on the wall. No one seemed to engage him.

Then the host responded. "That's all good, but it's too slow. Angeletti has a departure date, so this has got to move quickly. Do any of you know anybody in this town who could put Harry on the ropes? Any of you have an influential godfather you'd be willing to share?"

"Louie Gargaston," someone said.

There was a gasp.

The host looked around the room for the voice, settling on the director of academic exchanges. "You mean you can deliver Gargaston?"

"I think so. Look, what we all know but aren't saying is that this isn't about Angeletti. It's bigger than that. All the political appointees in the building are demoralized because if Cone will fire a friend with a good idea who's doing a good job, then what will he do to us?"

The remark resonated across the room. Feet shuffled. People said "right!" nodding their heads.

Jason was amused by the unintended inference that maybe they weren't doing that good a job themselves. He was beginning to feel like a pawn in a chess game and impulsively said, "Who is Louis Gargaston anyway?"

The host looked up with impatience. "He's commissioner of public properties."

Jason shot back. "Never heard of him!"

People rustled their feet again.

"That's just the point." The host was getting animated. "He doesn't want anything to do with publicity or notoriety. That's why he told the president he'd only come to Washington if he were given something under the radar screen. The president thinks a lot of Gargaston and uses him for advice and troubleshooting. In fact, Louie has named half the cabinet. He keeps an eye on things, and he's good at it, too. Only thing is, he's been investigated for a violation of the Hatch Act, but even that didn't get out to the press."

Jason pressed. "What's the Hatch Act?"

People shuffled their feet again, and someone scraped their heel on the floor.

"That says you're not supposed to work for any political party while you're on the federal payroll. But the only way Louie can keep in touch with all the state conventions is during business hours."

The taxi pulled up to a brownstone in a residential section. Jason was ushered into a large room on the first floor with an old fireplace near the door. In the left corner of the room was a giant desk next to a telephone switchboard. Seated behind it was a huge man in his sixties who weighed at least three hundred and fifty pounds. He wore a shoestring bow tie and was sitting in an enormous swivel chair made from two others. In both of his ears were plugs connected directly to the switchboard. He removed them when he saw Jason.

"Well, well, is this the fellow I've been told about? Let's see, it's Jason Angel-something, isn't it?" The large man extended his fleshy hand across the table without getting up.

As Jason grabbed it, he felt like he was sliding into a catcher's mitt.

"It's Angeletti, sir. Jason Angeletti."

"Well, are you an angel, Jason? Because if you are, you have no business working for Harry Cone. Tell me, how on earth did you ever meet him?"

"I gave him piano lessons when I was an undergraduate student some ten years ago."

"Oh, yes, Harry and the piano. He must have been a difficult student, very impatient and a short attention span. Did he ever practice?"

"Not really."

"I'm not surprised. You know, Harry Cone has a lot of personnel problems right now. I'm working on some of them. There are people in the radio broadcasting section who are ready to shoot each other. Tell me exactly how and when you were fired."

"It was yesterday morning. My superior, Rollie Lovemore, associate director of the agency, handed me a letter telling me I was axed."

"Did Harry sign the letter?"

"No, it was from Rollie Lovemore."

"Who else was involved?"

"I believe Bonita Baracuddle from the arts office in another bureau..."

"Have you seen Harry or discussed this with him since you received the letter?"

"No."

"Tell me, if we get you back in, what would you like?"

"Sorry?"

"I mean what kind of job do you want? Deputy director?" Jason couldn't believe his ears. Deputy director of the whole damn agency? Boy, that would shock some people. "No, sir, not really. I just want to continue what I'm doing right now."

"You mean this little music program they told me about?"

Jason nodded.

"Well, here's what I suggest. First, we have to find out whether Harry even knew about this."

"Oh, I'm sure he did," scoffed Jason. "I assume so anyway."

"Don't assume anything in this town." Gargaston spoke the words with razor sharpness. "Look, I'll call Harry Cone and set up a meeting between the two of you. And, because Harry's a pretty rough guy, I'd better go along with you. Do you have any objection to that?"

"No."

"And no time is better than the present. Let's see; it's past close of business. Do you have Harry's home phone number?"

"No, I've never called him there."

Louie reached for a phone. "I'll call him on the White House signal line. I guarantee he'll pick up." He flicked a switch at his desk that turned on some large speakers. Even the ring of the telephone could be heard clearly throughout the room. The telephone rang five times before Harry's unmistakable voice answered at the same time he picked up the receiver.

"Hello?"

"Harry, this is Louie Gargaston."

"Yeah, Louie."

"Gotta personnel problem here that I want to talk to

you about."

"Go ahead."

"Are you acquainted with Rollie Lovemore?'

"Yes, I am."

"Are you acquainted with a Bonita Baracuddle?"

"Somewhat."

"And are you acquainted with Jason Angeletti?"

"Yes, I know him very well."

"Are you aware that Jason Angeletti has been fired?"

"Yes."

"Would you agree to a meeting between the three of us to discuss this problem?"

"No, it's not necessary. I've been fully briefed on the matter, and that's my decision."

"Goodbye then, Harry."

Louie Gargaston was surprised. He looked up at Jason. "I'm sorry," he said in measured tones. "There's nothing more I can do."

Three of them sat gloomily around the dinner table.

"It's outrageous," said Marilyn, with a slight lisp. She looked at the two men who had just been fired. "We came to do the president's bidding," she said raising her glass at the mention of high office. "But we're surrounded by traitors."

Neither man responded.

She felt reproached and changed the subject. "It's lovely wine, really." Her tiny voice strained to be heard over the Dvorak *Requiem* playing through the stereo speakers. "Is it made in a free country?"

"Portugal." O'Rourke kept looking at the table.

"How about Chinese beer?" she asked, almost shouting as the

music reached a climax. "Do you drink that even though it's made by slaves?"

O'Rourke ignored her and looked at Jason. "Only one thing left for you, a 'Hail Mary' pass."

"I'm no good at football." Jason shrugged.

O'Rourke kept going. "You've got to set up an appointment to see Harry. There's nothing else left. The question is how to prepare for that meeting. You'll need advice." O'Rourke looked into the distance. "I've got it. A Catholic mystic!"

"What's that?"

"A holy man... prays all day. There's one here in town, Father O'Malley. I don't know how a monk who spends his days shut up in a walled priory can know so much about human nature, but they say he's preternaturally smart. Few people know he's here, and he's very hard to get to see. But I might be able to work it."

As he drove up to the monastery in Northeast Washington, Jason did not know exactly what he wanted from Father O'Malley—maybe a mass or a blessing or even a miracle. He rang the bell, and the great wooden doors opened slowly with an anguished creak.

It was Brother Ernie who welcomed him in silence. He beckoned Jason to follow across the marble floor past the forbidding life-sized statues of the saints into a small anteroom furnished with two chairs, a table, a lamp, and a window. Brother Ernie left with a slight bow, and Jason sat there alone, mesmerized by the complete silence.

Then, from a distance, he heard quick footsteps growing closer. A small man whisked into the room, wearing the robes of a religious habit, both hands crossed in front of the other and buried in the furls of the opposite sleeve.

"Since I was told about you, I saw something in the news about the ICCA. I, of course, thought of you, Jason." The old priest came to the point with the utmost gentleness.

Jason felt comfortable. They chatted for a few moments, and soon Jason began reiterating his experiences of the past several months, culminating in his firing. "And I have a meeting with Harry Cone tomorrow, Father. I don't know what I'm going to say or even why I was fired. I guess I'll just have to show up." Jason tried to hide his nervousness.

The priest took a long breath, folded his hands, then put them back into his sleeves. He gazed out the window. "For the children of this world are more astute in dealing with their own kind than are the children of light. Behold, you are like lambs among wolves."

"I beg your pardon, Father?"

"The Gospel of Saint Luke," said the priest, still looking out the window.

Jason was distracted by a distant noise, perhaps the clatter of something falling on the floor. Everything could be heard with breathtaking clarity in this house of peace.

"At least Harry agreed to see you. That's something anyway."

"I suppose so," said Jason.

"He may even be curious about how you're doing. He might ask you. You could say you were fine until you were fired." The priest chuckled softly.

"That's for sure." Jason wondered where all this was going.

"Harry might also say, 'Well, you made a lot of enemies.'" Here, the priest paused. "And you could say to him, 'Well, Harry, we all have enemies, don't we?'"

Jason muttered something innocuous about never having seen so many enemies.

But the priest continued. "And Harry would think your enemies were becoming his, and he already has enough." Father O'Malley looked directly at Jason and, with an engaging smile, said, "The correct answer to that is that any man in Harry's position will have enemies, which is all the more reason not to fire his friends. But Harry may not under-stand the word 'friend' in the same way you do, Jason."

"What do you mean?"

"Well, he may feel that a friend is someone who can do something for him. And there, Jason, you're in a weak position."

"What about my credentials, my qualifications, Father? Doesn't that reflect well on my appointment?"

"Objectively speaking, yes. But I would imagine the world Harry lives in now is so cutthroat that qualifications do not matter—only power."

Jason silently rejected this notion.

"But if you bring up your credentials, Jason, it may remind Harry of your skills as his former teacher, skills which he admired. He may even feel he owes it to you to come clean about why you were fired."

"Well, that would be interesting." Jason tried to conceal his impatience.

"At this point, you might even learn whether Harry really wanted to fire you or not. But if he shows any concern for what you will do in the future—"

Jason interrupted to say he had already resigned his teaching position at the university.

"Be sure and tell Harry that," said the monk. "And if he shows any sympathy, think of ways you can build on that by getting him support to overcome the people who are against you."

Jason listened dutifully, out of respect, but left feeling disappointed. That night, he slept well with the peculiar peace of mind that comes with unmitigated and complete failure.

Harry's outer office was frenetic as usual. Fax machines were sputtering, secretaries were tearing paper out of typewriters, and copy machines were collating mountains of nonsense. It looked like a feeding frenzy of white bonded paper. But this time, there was no waiting. The appointment secretary smiled and told Jason to go right in. Harry was on the phone but got off almost immediately. He walked to a couch and sat, facing Jason but not looking at him. As he absently brushed lint from his pant leg, he said, "How are you doing?"

"I thought I was doing fine, until I was fired," Jason found himself saying.

"Well, you made a lot of enemies."

"We all have enemies, don't we?"

"But your enemies are becoming my enemies, and I have enough enemies."

"Any man in your position will have enemies which is all the more reason not to fire his friends."

The cycle of rapid-fire conversation was broken for a moment as Harry peered at Jason. "What could you possibly do for me?"

"What about my credentials? If anybody is qualified to do what they're doing, it's me," said Jason.

"Credentials don't mean anything," replied Harry. "I hired a woman who had degrees in international law and spoke three languages. Because she was short of cash at the time and worked in a delicatessen, I got hit over the head with it." Harry grimaced and shrugged. "Look, Jason, people are saying that I've got my piano teacher on the payroll. They're gonna try and blow this thing up with leaks to the papers. They'll say that you shouldn't really be running a program like this."

"It makes me look like some guy in an attic that comes down for crumbs," said Jason.

"What are you going to do now, go back and teach at that university?"

"No. I already resigned my teaching position there. I don't know what I'm going to do now."

Harry's face hardened for a moment. Jason knew that Harry had probably been deceived.

"How can we reverse this?" the director asked.

Jason raced ahead. "Do you need support to ride this thing out?"

Harry almost jumped out of his seat. "Can you get me support?"

"I've been around a little, and I'm acquainted with some well-known musicians who can attest to my abilities."

"Have them write me immediately and mark the envelopes confidential. I'll give orders that any such letters should not go through the secretariat on the seventh floor but come directly into my office. How soon can they start arriving?"

"Four days," said Jason, settling on a round number. "And, by the way, I've got Marilyn Goodrump's support, too."

"Who in the hell is that?"

"She's acting director of the—"

"Never mind. Have fun while you're young. Good luck now, boy."

When six letters had arrived exactly four days later, Harry called a meeting. By the time the meeting was held, nine more letters had arrived. Gathered together were the top management of the agency: presidential appointees, career ministers, Mark Leduk, the counselor to the director, and the elite area directors of the Foreign Service.

"I'm against a review of this situation," said Rollie Lovemore. "There's already a paper trail here, and everybody could wind up being embarrassed."

"We can't allow the bureaucracy to push us around," Harry countered.

The meeting lasted one and a half hours, after which Jason Angeletti was rehired.

He called O'Rourke.

"Congratulations, Jason, and no offense, but if all that brass met for an hour and a half over your music program, what would they do if we ever went to war?"

CHAPTER FOUR

*T*he agency offices and corridors were ungodly quiet. The re-hiring of Jason Angeletti was against all laws of the natural world in government. No one could remember the dismemberment of an employee, with all the inviolable paperwork done for their departure, and then the verdict being reversed. It was like an out-of-body experience, empirical evidence that there was life after death; Lazarus had risen in their midst.

Preternaturally soothing, lavender sounds came through the window of Jason's one-room apartment on Capitol Hill. The storm of the middle section had subsided, leaving only delicate filigree as the Chopin nocturne floated like a soft dream around the walls of the room. Jason's fingers flattened. He returned to the main melody, kneading the keys as if making bread.

The richness of the sound and the flexibility of the line made Marilyn want to sing. It was all so natural. Then he played the final cadence like a whisper, as though life was being extinguished. After the sound died, he remained still for a moment, then looked up. Marilyn was crying.

"I've never heard anything so beautiful," she said, wiping her eyes. "I can't believe it. You should be going on one of those musical emissary trips yourself."

He nodded as though to himself. "Maybe someday." His voice was far off. He desperately wanted to play overseas but had to bide his time. The moment would come, but for now, he wanted to change the subject. "Thanks for dinner tonight. The Jockey Club's pretty special."

"Oh, Jason, we just had to celebrate your rehiring. Did you like the place?" She was trying to compose herself.

"Sure. And swanky, too."

"Look," she said, standing up. "You have to give a concert. I've never heard you play before. Others have to hear you. It will put an end to this 'piano teacher, crony' stuff."

"Where?"

"The Kennedy Center of course."

"That's big."

"You're big, and what you're trying to do is big. There's got to be a way. I'm going to look into it."

Jason felt even more attracted to her. He crossed the room to touch her face, and they held each other.

Jason's rehiring was specially celebrated in the Office of Personal Exchange. Marilyn had arranged for a cake and some wine.

One of the thirty people in the office told him, "Everybody feels you're one of us now. Cone's fired everybody but his wife and finally you. Now you're on the outs like the rest of us."

One of the office secretaries interrupted. "Mr. Angeletti, there's a call from Mr. Hinchmin's office. He wants to see you right away."

Jason raced to the eighth floor. Nate Hinchmin's suite of offices in administration and personnel was down the hall from Harry's, with access and size befitting a presidential appointee.

"Jason, let me say personally that I'm glad things worked out. Mark Leduk told Mr. Cone that you should be given a departure date two weeks hence, and I said that was unconscionable. We managed to string it out for a couple of months and look what happened." His voice was gelid and monotone.

Jason looked for some betrayal of warmth behind the wire-rim glasses, but there was none, only a new piece of information: Leduk was involved in his firing.

"Today, we have several things to cover," he continued. "First, regarding adjudicating the auditions, the director wants you to travel with a consultant who is 'professionally recognized as a musician.'"

Jason winced; he suddenly felt illegitimate.

"Secondly, he has asked me to make it clear that you will have to rely less on him and more on the cooperation of the bureaucracy for success. And lastly, the director has decided you need some staff help for your program. How many people do you think you need to do the national competition and then the overseas programming?"

"Three more."

"Okay. How about an assistant, a program coordinator, and a secretary?"

"Great!"

"But before you can start interviewing, it will take several months to advertise and fulfill all necessary hiring regulations. So we'd like to put someone in your office on temporary detail in order to bridge that gap. Her name is Margaret Ditherspoon." He handed Jason her résumé. There was nothing on it except references from party chieftains.

"Will she work out?" Jason was skeptical.

Hinchmin's face clouded. "We're doing you a favor."

When she reported for work the next day, Margaret was shown her office and asked for an ashtray. Over the next few days, her chain-smoking and the fluorescent lighting gave her small cubicle an unhealthy pallor.

Jason suggested that smoking was not good for her health. He didn't mention it might be even worse for someone in her middle sixties. Their first fight was over her typing, which was minimal. The second was over her filing system. Margaret used only colored labels: red was for miscellaneous, blue for music, and yellow was for everything else. He showed her résumé to Marilyn.

"There's nothing we can do," she said, "except wait it out. Anyway, she's billed herself as a superb fundraiser, Jason. You'll need that money for the large congressional reception you're planning when the finalists come to Washington. George Ogerthorpe already said that this money can only come from private funding. Margaret promised to arrange it, plus the room, invitations, and the caterer."

It took Margaret two days and four packs of cigarettes to type the draft letter using one finger. Jason finally got all the new letters sent out to contestants, assigning dates and times for their auditions. He looked at a large map on the wall in his office. The audition sites were strategically located so people would not have to travel far. He turned his concentration on finding a consultant to go with him.

Wendell Marchant, a tall, somewhat rotundish, brilliant, bald seventy-four-year-old, was a retired music critic of the *Washington Post* and *Star*. Jason discovered he had three doctorates from Columbia University: one in music composition, the second in music history, and the third in German philology. He was also a gourmet, an expert on the Civil War, played every instrument known to music, and had been a senior official in the U.S. Navy. It was in this latter capacity that he designed a textbook on naval gunnery that was still required reading at the Naval Academy in Annapolis. This guy was, indeed, "professional."

It ought to please Harry Cone, he thought. The next day, he called Dr. Marchant and then went to the budget office to authorize their travel orders.

It was probably the greatest trip that Wendell had ever taken. He crossed the great breadth of land for six weeks, listening to pianists and visiting places he had not seen in fifty years. At dinner, he would discuss the regional cuisine. In Boulder, Colorado, he introduced Jason to buffalo sausage, in Seattle, smoked fish, in New Orleans, crawfish étoufée, and in Boston, a certain scrod. On long flights, he regaled Jason with stories of American history, politics, music, frontier justice, and anything else that spilled from his encyclopedic mind.

Throughout, Wendell smoked unfiltered Camels, except when rolling his own cigarettes with pipe tobacco. Jason enjoyed his eccentricities and irreverence.

They had dinner at a pretentious hotel in Houston where the waiters were officious. The offerings were marinated roast duck with cilantro and lime, gently brushed with Dijon mustard. The vegetable was "whipped puff of caramelized yam."

Wendell quipped, "For desert, they'll tickle our balls."

Afterward, they rode back to the hotel with a petulant cab driver who wasn't in the mood to give his passengers a receipt. Wendell gave him a two-dollar tip with instructions that "it be spent on some liniment for that pain in your ass."

During the auditions in Boston, an ultra-modern composition was presented by a man who climbed halfway into the harp of the grand piano and began plucking the strings with his right hand while, as Wendell said, "picking his nose with the left."

At a bar in Texas, the proprietor wanted them to try the local beer. Wendell blew the suds off the mug and sipped it. "Your horse has diabetes," he said.

Besides being a pleasant companion, Wendell also proved indispensable as a judge. Jason was impressed with his broad knowledge of the repertoire and awareness of what kind of playing projected to an audience.

He was pleased that the auditions had gone well for such a grand, logistical venture. The budget was small with mostly donated facilities, but it worked. Above all, there appeared to be no disgruntled people among the contestants. Thank God! Jason was convinced that, if Harry had gotten any kind of negative letters, he would have considered the whole adventure a liability. And, above all, they had chosen artists for the finals who would auger well for the program. Pianists came out of the woodwork, flocking from every corner of the country. Jason knew they would, as he would have.

The trip wound down in Tucson, Arizona, where Wendell and Jason checked into the Arizona Inn for a few days. They had their limit of finalists—fourteen—and now had a chance to relax by the pool, do their laundry, and stroll around the grounds. That evening, he walked through an avenue of palm trees to Wendell's bungalow, where they split a six-pack of beer.

"Wendell, you've been in the government. You know what it's like. Why are they after me?"

"Because you're different. It's like a rooster in with a bunch of hens; they'll try to peck you to death. The bureaucracy's a different culture, with different standards and rules of conduct. Even Harry's finding that out."

"What should I do?"

"Don't be too nice or saintly, or they'll keep kicking you in the stomach. Then you'll get ulcers, and that's a sin, too."

"What about the politicals?"

"Well, some of them will wind up not liking you because you break their rules, too. See, there are basically three types of political appointees. First, the policy boys that keep coming back whenever their political party is in power. There are about one or two thousand of them around, mostly in Washington. They have the experience, know how the game is played, and rotate into cabinet or other high-level positions every decade or so. Secondly, there are the heavy contributors. They usually wind up with ambassadorships or sitting in on blue ribbon commissions. Finally, there are the relatives of administration officials and cronies. They're not supposed to do anything except sit and collect a nice paycheck they couldn't get anywhere else. In some people's minds, you probably fit into this last category—except you actually did something. In fact, you rocked the boat."

"So what?"

"This is a real sensitive agency. You've got the career civil servants, a plethora of political appointees, and then the Foreign Service, all with competing agendas that have nothing to do with the guy at the top. Those are real divergent elements and make for a lethal combination."

"Is every administration like this?"

"Different clowns, same circus. Maybe this one's got a few more elephants and giraffes."

"Where will the greatest danger come from?"

"Dunno, maybe the Foreign Service."

"Why?"

"Because they know a great deal about things that aren't so."

Marilyn met them at the airport. She was overjoyed to see Jason in the wake of his triumphant return. It amazed her that the thing had gone off without a hitch, without any of the myriad complications that can turn taxpayer's money into a scandal or public rebuke. She felt a part of it. And she was beginning to feel a part of Jason as well. This was an entirely new experience for her.

"There's so much news, Jason. They finally replaced Ed O'Rourke, so I'm back to being a lowly deputy again." She feigned a pouty face, then smiled. "Clark Krieg, the new office director, wants to see you first thing in the morning, and Margaret Ditherspoon hasn't raised a penny for the reception. She's been out of the office a lot, too. Migraines, I guess... and the agency magazine did a story about the audition... and I might have found a sponsor for your concert at the Kennedy Center... and..." She spoke breathlessly until they got to the curb. Jason and Dr. Marchant waited with their luggage while Marilyn went to get the car.

"She should be your deputy, not somebody else's." Wendell raised his eyebrows in his companion's direction. "If it were me, I'd want her around all the time."

Jason tried to deflect the subject with some grace. "I see you appreciate beauty in all forms."

"I may be old, but I'm not dead."

The lobby of the agency seemed so confining after the broad expanses of land Jason had just traversed; it seemed uptight and artificial. Some of the people milling around congratulated him on the auditions. A man in the elevator even mentioned the article in the agency's magazine. "Terrific," he said. Jason thanked him and got out at the third floor, rounding the corner toward the new office director's suite. Go right in," said the secretary.

Clark Krieg stood from behind his desk and motioned toward a sofa and chairs. Introductions were not necessary. They had both heard about each other. "Found any good people out there?"

"Yup!" Jason studied Clark. It was apparent he was not the defiant, rallying figure that Edmund O'Rourke was. Flat-footed, academic, and of medium height, his hair was arranged in such a way as to conceal his almost complete baldness. He had let it grow long on one side in order to comb it over the top. But his movements were jerky, and when he turned his head quickly to one side, the hair did not immediately follow.

"I've heard you've been through the mill." Dr. Kreig's head turned rapidly to the left, where it remained stationary for a split second, and then a short, almost violent nod before returning to its normal position.

"It was a near-run thing," Jason said, staring at Kreig. He wished Marilyn had warned him about the facial tics.

"Whew, what a pressure cooker!" Clark's head made a full circle as though watching something fly through the air. "Listen, we have to talk about Margaret Ditherspoon. Is she any good?"

"A disaster."

"That's what I've heard, but we can't get rid of her altogether. We don't want any trouble from Louie Gargaston."

Jason looked surprised.

"Yeah, he's called Harry." At the mention of Harry Cone's name, Clark Kreig turned his head to the left and brought his shoulder up to meet his chin in a quick waltz rhythm. "He probably knows she's marginal and needs protection. We'll give her a job keeping everybody's Rolodex in order." Clark suddenly grew more serious. "Close the door."

Jason looked around for interlopers as he reached for the doorknob.

Kreig's voice was a hush. "Mark Leduk has begun a purge of midlevel political appointees. I think it's to further isolate Harry Cone. He's arguing that, in the wake of the Babygate scandal, it would be a sign of good faith to Congress if the agency fired many of their already-too-numerous political appointees." Kreig's head made a full circle. "When I heard about it, I knew Marilyn Goodrump would be on their list." His head made another circle but in the opposite direction.

"Make her my deputy," Jason said immediately. "And at the same pay level as an office deputy director. Nobody will object since I'm on a roll right now, and the director knows I need a staff. She fits the bill, and it'll avoid anything messy for them."

The tics stopped for a moment, and Kreig smiled. "I think we can do that."

He took Marilyn dancing at the Jockey Club that night and tried to tell her the news gently. They moved across the smooth dance floor with the same understated elegance as their surroundings. Dark wood paneling, soft lights, and the refined gracefulness of flowers and large paintings dominated the room. Marble pillars bordered the dance floor, and waiters in waistcoats moved almost invisibly along the periphery delivering cocktails to small tables. The pianist played Gershwin.

"I had no choice. It was a *fait accompli.*"

She furled her brows quizzically.

"French! That means it was a done deal. I wanted to save you from the long knives. You know… the purge!" He searched her eyes for a reaction. The pianist played a soft, velvet arpeggio while Jason held Marilyn against his cheek. "You'll make the same amount of money." He still hadn't hit the right spot. "You don't mind working with me, do you?"

She stopped and peered into his eyes. "I love what you're doing." She kissed him lightly, then started shaking.

"What's wrong?"

"Power," she said. "There's a flip side to it, isn't there? Possible annihilation!"

Jason thought they were both growing up.

It was only two weeks before the real show would begin—the third and final round of auditions at the Library of Congress. The rest of his staff had still not been chosen because their job vacancy postings were dragging on. So he and Marilyn put in fourteen-hour days, trying to nail down the logistics of bringing fourteen pianists from as many states into Washington, D.C. Now that Harry had authorized a federal advisory ICCA panel, Jason had three well-known judges coming. This meant there were grants to be filled out and authorized, per diem checks cut, hotel reservations made, and practice facilities arranged.

"What are we going to do about money for the congressional reception?" Marilyn asked. "We haven't raised any, and the lawyers said it can't be done on public money."

Jason sent an action memo to Harry, requesting some of the director's discretionary funds.

Bill Barron came back with a curt reply, "Get out of this on your own."

Panic set in. If one component of the program failed, it could send everything else into a tailspin. Jason sent an all-points bulletin to his political brethren in the bureau.

The director of the Overseas Guest Program responded: "We all want this to succeed, Jason, so get in touch with Luddie Twelfth-Night. He should be good for the whole thing."

"Who?"

"Ludlow Twelfth-Night III. I'll give you his number. He's got a little pied-à-terre in Georgetown. I'll call him first."

"Who is this guy?"

"Twelfth-Night Cream Sherry empire, Jason. The guy's got

millions, and he wants to be important. That's all you need to know."

Jason was amazed at how easy it was to set up the meeting. Luddie said he wanted to meet in the lounge bar of the Four Seasons Hotel at 4:00 p.m. the next day. Jason always wanted to go there. It had a subdued, comfortable atmosphere in the heart of Georgetown. The lounge bar was an open seating area with plush sofas, potted palms, and small tables for drinks. The maître d' took him to Mr. Twelfth-Night's table near the window overlooking a canal.

"They tell me you really believe in this thing, kid. Do you know how rare that is in this town?"

Jason noticed Luddie spoke through clenched teeth in a kind of lockjaw style that smacked of yachts, polo shirts, Ivy League reunions, and money. They drank cocktails and ate finger food for about four hours. Jason tried to stay awake while Luddie felt compelled to express every thought he had ever had and then drop a multitude of names.

"I told the president I would accept the ambassadorship to England, but Maime and I would have to have the whole residence redone. I mean, who wants to live in a place that's early Howard Johnson? We'd been guests there too many times, and Maime finally said, 'No, it's just too sticky!'"

When Luddie paused to scrape some food off his Yale tie, Jason jumped into the conversation. "I wonder if you'd like to help fund my program?"

Luddie peered at Jason and moved close to him—uncomfortably so, like a lover. "Look, kid, I'm not a fringe person. Do you understand? When I do something, I'm on the inside. Now, you set up a meeting between Harry Cone and me. I want to see how serious he is about this thing. I mean, I'm careful."

"All right, I'll try. But I've got to get some help for this congressional reception. We're bringing all these pianists back here for the final round of the competition."

"You mean you need some stuff for your dog and pony show. Okay, kid, I'll give you a case of wine. And you know why I'm gonna do this? Because you really believe in this thing. Do you know how rare that is in this town?"

The bill came, and Jason read it upside down while Luddie whipped out a gold credit card. It was $425.

The next day, Jason walked cautiously, as always, through the outer lobby of Harry's office toward the director's half-open door. He felt like an Indian scout walking through the brush, trying not to step on a twig. He convinced himself none of the all-seeing eyes would notice him. When he got to Harry's door, he opened it wider as the executive secretary gave out a passively hostile sigh.

He saw Harry carrying memoranda in each hand, moving his head back and forth trying to read both. Jason noticed Harry moved his lips while he read. Maybe this was a bad time, but Harry needed to know that Jason was making progress. "I've got Luddie Twelfth-Night III of Twelfth-Night Cream Sherry interested in helping out with the program," he said proudly.

Harry looked up, rearing his head like it had antlers. He focused over his reading glasses. "Check him out!"

"Check him out?" Jason didn't understand.

"You heard me, check him out!"

He stopped by Bill Barron's office. "What does the director mean when he says to check somebody out?"

"Go see Hinchmin," said Barron. "He'll know what to do."

Jason walked around the corner to the Bureau of Administration and Personnel.

"Can you get me his social security number?" Hinchmin was ready to write on a pad.

"Social Security number?"

"How about his wife's maiden name?" The questions were rapid-fire.

"Of course I can't. I just met the man. What's this all about?"

"FBI check."

"Nate, we're talking about a case of wine!"

"Harry said check him out, and that's what he means. Do you know any other angle? Has he had any contact with the White House?"

Jason was incredulous. "He told me he could've been ambassador to England, but didn't take it."

"Great, the White House ought to have a whole file on him then."

It was about five days later that Nate Hinchmin called Jason. "Luddie Twelfth-Night's never been asked to be an ambassador. The only thing they can find is that he contributed a thousand dollars to the presidential campaign."

Luddie called Jason's office the next day.

"I know what you're trying to do, you and Harry Cone. I've got my contacts around town. You people called the White House to see if I'm a fringe person. Well, I'm not a fringe person. The case of wine is off!"

The story about Luddie went through the office like a prairie fire.

Marilyn Goodrump was disgusted. "What a bust!" She volunteered to organize some of the women from the Office of Personal Exchange to help Jason pull off the reception. "Even if it turns out to be potluck, we'll manage, Jason."

Her reassurance was a balm. It was one less thing to worry about. He gratefully wrote out a personal check for the wine.

"You don't have to do that."

"Why not?" he said. "It'll help, and besides, if there's not enough sauvignon blanc, Harry might fire me again."

"Shelley will help, and she knows wine."

Jason wrinkled his nose. "Shelley? You mean Harry Cone's chief sycophant."

Shelley Fatchawada was a fiftyish, Italianate New Yorker who was squat, noisy, and attired in loud silks. She made it a point to work hard at gaining close access to Harry Cone.

"We need her," said Marilyn.

"Why? She's just a cocktail waitress for Harry Cone's friends."

Marilyn admonished him. "Jason, the private get-together committees, which Shelley handles, are full of important and successful people who Mr. Cone knows personally. They're supposed to volunteer their advice on how best to sell America overseas."

"Their advice is probably selling America down the river."

"We need her!" Marilyn blinked rapidly.

He went downstairs to the printing office to work on the program booklet for the auditions, including the evening ceremony. For the speeches, he landed a congressman, several

high-level bureaucrats, and Wendell Marchant. He asked
Harry's office about availability, but they said the director was
already booked. Each of the speakers was listed in bold foil
lettering in the booklet, as well as the contestants, their repertoire, a biography, and the day and time of their audition. He
also procured a shuttle to take agency employees over to the
Library of Congress on an hourly basis. Everything was
coming together. The grants had been processed for the finalists, and their plane tickets had been sent. Hotel reservations
were already secured as well as practice times at a nearby
university music school, all on the same travel line of the
underground metro. Jason had the press section of the agency
send out notices to the media, while Marilyn worked with the
congressional office inviting senators and congressmen from
the states the finalists came from.

At close of business, Jason called his parents in the Midwest.
"You might want to come to this," he said. "And if you do,
could you bring some cheese in a cooler? We'll need some for
the reception."

The morning of the competition was bright and clear. There
had been a leak over the closet in his little apartment on
Capitol Hill, and he was up half the night. It had taken a long
time to move everything out since most of his worldly goods
were deposited there. And then there was the steady drip into
the pail all night. His place was not ideal, but his lease was a

month-to-month rental agreement, and this made him feel secure in case he was fired again. So when he awoke, his clothes and books were strewn over chairs and on the floor; but that wasn't the only thing that made him feel unsettled this chilly November morning. He fretted over details of the day. He finished dressing, made a cup of instant coffee, found his overcoat in a heap on the floor, and left the building for the short walk up the hill.

As he crossed D Street, a cold blast of air made him rearrange his scarf. He was more alert now as the majestic edifice of the Jefferson Building, of the Library of Congress, came into view. He was glad he had gotten so many agency employees on detail assignment to help him and Marilyn through the next two days; it would be good to have them around for support. His mind went over everything again; it seemed there was always something. He crossed Pennsylvania Avenue and realized that no one had arranged parking privileges.

As he entered the building, employees of the Library were setting up entrance procedures with the security guards. He walked past them and turned down the marble corridor to the beautiful and historic auditorium. He looked in and saw the piano on center stage with the lid up in concert position. He tried it to see if it was in tune. An audio crew from the broadcasting section of the agency was setting up microphones and tape decks. He felt a sense of relief that things were coming together. *This might actually work*, he thought.

He spotted his friend Merlina Oyassis, who was one of those

on detail. Her job was to log all the contestants in. Then, people from the press section of the agency started showing up. Marilyn Goodrump had been there since before sunup, arranging tables in the marble corridor with literature about the agency and the Musical Emissary Program. A library employee came to open two side rooms. One had a grand piano for the contestants to warm up, and the other was for the Foreign Service interviews. Jason prided himself on that idea —a bone to throw the diplomats. They would ask the contestants some questions to find out if the musicians could properly put an English sentence together. But the Foreign Service didn't have a vote; that was key. The idea succeeded, however, in mobilizing support amongst the corps.

Next came the announcer who was a program officer from Clark Kreig's office. Then the judges appeared, three of them together, and, finally, the two Foreign Service interviewers. It was only 8:30 a.m., and yet something was in place that the agency historian told him had never been accomplished before in government.

Merlina winked at him. "This is just like downtown, Jason. Is Harry Coney-poo coming to hear these wonderful people play, or would he be too jealous?"

"He won't be here, but he'll be at the reception tonight."

"Good," she said. "Then we can all have fun until then."

The contestants began showing up, and music wafted from the warm-up room. Everyone was excited. It didn't seem like the government anymore. At exactly 9:30 a.m., the announcer took to the stage and greeted the judges and the few scattered spectators, who had heard of the event through the library's circular or had come on the agency's shuttle. He announced the first contestant and the repertoire to be performed. At 9:35 a.m., the competition began to the strains of a Bach prelude. The playing was excellent. Jason sat in the back row with a smile.

It was after lunch, at about 2:15 p.m., that a young nominee from Brigham Young University was performing Liszt's Hungarian Rhapsody, No. 12. Merlina Oyassis quietly sidled up next to Jason. He could smell her perfume.

"Jason?" she whispered.

"Yes."

"Contestant number five from Dallas is trapped under the stage."

Jason looked at her. "You're kidding! That's impossible."

"For you and me, it's impossible. But security just called and said that for Farley Martin from Dallas, it isn't. I figure he's either too chickenshit to get up there and play, or he's really lost under the stage."

"How did he get in touch with security?"

"It was pitch black under the stage, so he groped around for something. He landed on a phone that was hooked up directly to security. I think they're coming any minute."

The doors swung open with a bang, startling the judges. Two men with big bellies, holstered guns, and police hats marched down the aisle and up onto the stage. The pianist continued in a cascading cadenza.

"Let's try it over here, Henry." The security guard unholstered his gun and banged the butt of it on the stage floor three times. The piano exploded with a roar of chromatic interlocking octaves. "Did you hear anything, Henry?"

"Nope."

"Over here then."

The pianist had begun the lively *czárdás* section. His hands were a blur.

"Help!"

"Where was that?"

"Over here quick, by the outlet."

"He's in the bloody boiler room."

"Let's get down there quick."

They exited stage left. Jason went around back and waited by the door to a subterranean passage leading down under the stage.

A few moments later, Farley Martin emerged with a ghostly-pale face, perspiring in his suit. "I'm so sorry, Mr. Angeletti. I hope this won't influence the judges. I hope I didn't disrupt anything or ruin my—I was just looking for the bathroom."

"Did you get to go?"

"My God! I forgot."

It was winding down. The last contestant of the day was finishing, and the press tables in front of the auditorium had been abandoned. He looked at his watch. People were already leaving for the reception, and it was time for him to go, too.

One of the Foreign Service interviewers walked up to him. "Got a minute?"

"Sure."

"These people are great. We've been talking to them all day, and we're impressed. But, there's one guy though who's a bit of a... well..."

"A banana?"

"Yeah."

"What did he say?"

"Okay, we worked out these little questions just to see how

they'd respond. And this guy's an old-timer. I mean, he's pushing sixty."

"Well, there's no age limit in the competition."

"Must not be. I think he's a professor or something. Anyway, we asked him what his greatest musical influences were as a youth. He answered that when he was a boy, he looked in the mirror and realized he was very tired. That was his answer! And every answer was like that. We asked him to what part of the world he would like to be sent if he were chosen as an emissary, and he said, anywhere he could rest. I mean, we have real questions about this guy. Does our vote count with the panel or what?"

"Your role is one of persuasion only, but it is an important one."

The officer looked grave, almost standing at attention.

"I understand. The stakes are high. We'll do our best to make it foolproof."

Jason felt sadness about the sixty-year-old pianist. Both he and Wendell Marchant had agreed the man was an extraordinary artist. He probably was tired if he was still auditioning at sixty.

The walk to the Rayburn House Office Building was across First Street SE and about four hundred yards down Pennsylvania Avenue. It was a prestigious place to have the reception. The building was one of those giant new office structures that Congress had named after itself. It was a real Washington walk, in the loop of power and prestige with the Capitol Building sitting across Independence Ave. Jason moved slowly, exhausted by his lack of sleep and the day's activities. The fatigue had extinguished any feelings; he was immune from worry. Shelley Fatchawada and the women from the Office of Personal Exchange were handling the details of the reception anyway, and his parents would be there.

They were driving in with a rented trailer filled with three cases of wine, wheels of swiss and cheddar cheeses, and smoked ham and sausages. Most of it had been paid for by Jason's father, but some had been donated by family friends from his hometown of Charmsville, Wisconsin. Ironic that Harry wouldn't give him the money. He tried to fight against a feeling of resentment.

As he got to the entrance of the House Office Building, he felt pride that congressmen and senators might actually come. He had no experience with these sorts of people, but Harry was extremely particular about how they were to be treated. Jason figured Shelley could handle that, too. She told Jason that she knew how to do things the way "Harry liked them." But what if nobody showed up?

He entered the building and asked the security guard for the room number on his invitation. He suddenly realized he had never seen the room. Maybe he should have paid more attention to this whole thing. The guard said it was a conference hearing room, and he should climb the stairs and turn left.

As he walked down the thick carpet over the designs of eagles and Roman insignias, he heard the rumble of conversation. His pulse quickened. He came to a large doorway and looked into the glare of television lights. People were moving past each other like targets in a shooting gallery, engaged in animated conversation. The tables had white cloths and were laden with cheeses, fruits, smoked meats, wine, and flower arrangements. Harry Cone was standing in front of a camera with Rollie Lovemore and other agency officials. Jason had only a few seconds to take this in before someone shouted, "There he is!"

Shelley Fatchawada moved around and through people as she bustled her way toward him, looking like a tank with Christmas decorations. "This way, Jason. There are so many people who want to meet you." She introduced one person after another, speaking quickly and with a strong New York accent. She came to a congressman. "This is our die-rek-ta of the program, congressman. Of course, the whole idea was Harry Cone's. He thought of it just to help all these wonderful musicians. Isn't that wonderful?"

"Wonderful," said the congressman.

Then she waltzed Jason to a corner of the room to meet a senator and his wife. "The senator represents one of our final-ists, Jason."

The senator looked at neither but at the camera behind them. "Yes, and we're here to wish that wonderful musician well."

"Wonderful," said Jason. He took Shelley by the arm. "Why are you telling them this was Harry's idea?"

"Look, Jason, this is the big time. Harry Cone is the die-rek-ta of the whole goddamn agency." She raised her right arm with a clenched fist. "We work for him. He must be known as the savior of American music. That's what he'd want, and if you know what's good for you, that's what you'll want, too."

"We work for the American people, Shelley, not Harry Cone."

"Are you nuts, Jason? You're really nuts, aren't you? I'm talkin' to somebody that's nuts." She flung her hands up in the air.

His mother came over. "For God's sake, go over and talk to Mr. Cone, would you? It's obvious that you're avoiding him."

"I hope he falls through the floor," said Jason.

Shelley overheard it and choked on an ice cube.

"Well then, I'll go over and talk to him, even if you won't."

Jason followed his mother out of the corner of his eye. Flash bulbs popped. The director's personal photographer was taking pictures of him for no apparent reason. He watched Harry greet her, then the two started talking.

Shelley Fatchawada moved in the same direction, waiting for

them to finish so she could take Harry around for introductions.

Suddenly, the room dimmed, leaving only the focused glare of
television lights. Something was about to happen.

Rollie Lovemore stepped into the center of it all. "Ladies and
gentlemen, welcome to this reception and welcome into the
world of great ideas—not mine, but Harry Cone's. This
program is his show, and we're all wonderfully proud of it.
And now, here he is, the director of the International Cultural
Communications Agency, Harry Cone."

"Thank you, Rollie. I would like to state publicly that I'm very
happy about the Musical Emissary Program."

Rollie Lovemore started to applaud, and others followed
suit.

"Happier with that," Harry continued, "than I am with Rollie
Lovemore."

Rollie's smile waned, and beads of perspiration formed on his
forehead. He stared straight ahead.

Harry smiled broadly. "Just kidding. You've got to keep these
people on their toes. Now, I'd like to talk about the person
who's going to make the Musical Emissary Program a reality.
I want to introduce to you a great man, a great human, a great
heart, a great mind, a great leader, and a great talent. Ladies
and gentlemen, Jason Angeletti."

Jason was embarrassed. He felt like he was at a Stalinist show trial.

A Foreign Service Officer whispered as Jason passed by, "Don't say anything negative about anybody."

Jason unbuttoned his suit coat and stuck his thumb behind his belt. That occupied one hand. He didn't know what to do with the other. "Ladies and gentlemen, cultural exchange is an effective tool of public diplomacy, and when you put it together with music, it's even better. Thank you all for coming." He went to a table and poured himself a glass of wine, then went out with Marilyn and his parents for dinner.

Chinatown was all too familiar. They went to his favorite restaurant just under the arch, and soon their table was ladened with bowls of steamed rice and his favorite dishes. But Jason was interested in something else.

"Mother, what did you and Harry Cone talk about?"

"Oh, I don't want to say."

"Why?"

"Because I'll get it wrong."

Jason's father intervened. "If you don't start eating this stuff, it'll get cold and stick together. The rice already looks like a gelatinous mass."

Jason took his fork and stabbed a piece of sweet-and-sour chicken. "Go ahead, Mother. What did he say?"

"No, really, it's nothing."

"Please, it might be helpful to me."

"Well, he said he had a lot of hassles and moles in his office."

"And?"

"I can understand the hassles."

"Yes."

"But I always thought a mole was a little animal. Mr. Cone said he has so many of them up there. I just wondered why he has all these little animals in his office."

"Then what?"

"I felt sorry for him. He's like a twelve-year-old boy. So I said, 'Mr. Cone, you're going to get criticized whether you do the right thing or the wrong thing. So, you might as well go ahead and do the right thing.'"

"What did he say?"

"He just stared at me with his mouth open and then said he wanted to have his picture taken with me."

The competition wound down during the late afternoon of the

next day. The judges and the Foreign Service interviewers left the auditorium to deliberate. They were to report back to Jason with their decisions before the ceremony began at 8:00 p.m. Up to two winners could be chosen.

People began taking their seats at 7:45 p.m. The television crew from the agency studios was already setting up. A lectern had been moved onto the stage, and fourteen chairs were set in a semicircle around the piano. At exactly 8:00 p.m., the congressman who would announce the winners came in with his wife and driver. At 8:10, the judges still hadn't returned. Jason decided to begin the proceedings anyway. Clark Kreig was introduced and thanked the announcer with such a violent jerk of his head that his neck cracked.

Jason nervously paced the foyer outside while the speakers droned on. At 8:30, he thought he heard footsteps. The three judges came in somewhat unsteadily with the Foreign Service interviewers bringing up the rear.

One of them handed Jason a note listing the results and whispered, "Sorry we're late. These guys drank like they were going to the electric chair."

The judges were shown to their seats as a letter was read from the president of the United States commending the program and them for their selflessness. They were introduced from the stage and stood in unison, surprisingly without any difficulty.

The contestants were introduced by name as well as the school or festival which nominated them. The audience, comprised mostly of agency employees, smiled broadly as each contestant came onto the stage.

The high point of the evening was when the congressman announced the winners. In a stentorian voice, he dramatically announced the names of each one as he opened the judge's envelopes. The results could not have been more politically correct: a woman who was part Cherokee and a man possessed of a remarkable ethnic lineage—English, Jewish, and Japanese. His name was Neville Yamamoto Bettelheim. One Foreign Service Officer proclaimed the multicultural pluralism to be a "stroke of genius."

Jason noted that since one of the judges had already had a stroke, perhaps they should turn in early.

CHAPTER FIVE

*M*ark Leduk drummed his fingers on the desk. He watched them as they got faster, one following the other. Was he typing or playing the piano? He didn't know. He had piano lessons as a child but hadn't played in years. There were other things he didn't know, too. He pushed his chair back and walked over to the window. Cars crawled down Constitution Avenue past the National Mall. He looked at the Lincoln monument in the distance, then back at his desktop and wondered if he could still play a scale. He wondered too, how in the hell the Musical Emissary Program got as far as it did. He shook his head and looked up at the "Rogue's Gallery." That was the nickname his staff had given the wall of photographs of Mark and the president, Mark and the vice-president, Mark with senators, congressmen, ambassadors, and movie stars. Leduk liked famous people. His personal index of life held that people were famous because they deserved to be and the converse, that those who had not "made it" were probably losers. Who in the hell was Jason Angeletti anyway? He tugged angrily at the silk handkerchief in the breast pocket of his cashmere blazer. "Ramona," he bellowed into the intercom, "come and take some dictation, an eyes-only memo. And then hand carry it to each of the area directors."

Memorandum from: Mark Leduk, Counselor to the Director

To: Directors of the American Republics, Europe, Asia, Near East Asia, and Australia

Gentlemen: Despite the recent success of the Musical Emissary Program auditions, there remain dark corners to be aware of. Because part of the criteria for the musicians selected involves their not being well known or experienced but nevertheless representing the United States abroad, there remains the possibility that they will embarrass themselves and the country. We have a long tradition of sending only the best talent overseas to fulfill our mission. It is imperative that should these artists prove to be less, we reduce any further risk to the agency or American public diplo-macy by canceling their tours, even if they are in progress. Furthermore, it should be stated succinctly in the evaluation cable from the individual posts that this program is not desirable as an effective means of public diplomacy.

Edmund O'Rourke's war council started on time. Some had gotten there early and took seats on the sofa or the Parsons chair or other mismatched antiques, but most stood in the small living room. Ed had put on ballet music from Verdi's *Macbeth,* hoping to lighten the mood during what would be a somber discussion. But the Roman heaviness of the brass was anything but airy. He began the meeting with a hearty welcome and a smile that did not fit with the dance around the witch's cauldron filtering over the speakers.

"Well, here we are again. This time, it's twenty… TWENTY political appointees who have gotten their pink slips since Mark Leduk's 'reign of terror!' This man must be stopped!" O'Rourke slammed his fist on the arm of the old chair, which promptly cracked.

People pretended not to notice.

"It is outrageous that the president's own people are being hung out to dry. I propose a memo to the director signed by all office directors in the bureau alerting him to this fact."

"He'd never get it," someone shouted. "Rollie Lovemore would never let it go through, and even if it did, Bill Barron would intercept it in the director's office. Leduk had Barron go around to all the associate directors of the bureaus and ask them for a list of political appointees who could prove a liability to the director. Those are the twenty who have already bit the dust."

A macabre waltz filled the air as the third act closed.

Someone else spoke. "I've taken a survey of everybody here. We've done the usual: leaked it to staffers on the hill and called reporters and TV. We'll just have to wait and see what comes down."

The director of the Overseas Guest Program shook his head. "This time, there's one thing that's different. Remember poor old Margaret Ditherspoon? Turns out the reason she's never had anything on her résumé is that she's a Capitol Hill baby… been the kept mistress of at least two congressmen. She knows more people than we do. Of all the people that have been fired, Louie Gargaston is most unhappy about her. This time, there could be some retribution."

Congressman Bromide and his chief of staff pulled up to the gate of Harry Cone's luxurious home in Northwest Washington. One of them rolled the window down and shouted into a box. The security system activated, and flood lights went on, revealing a deep canyon descending to a river gorge on the left side of the house. A voice from the speaker box told them to remain stationary. A brawny man wearing a private security uniform came up to the driver's side to check identification.

"Is the president here tonight, or is something big going on?" asked the younger man.

"Nope, just a quiet evening for Director Cone." The guard's face was leathery.

"Why all this security then? Who'd want to shoot Harry Cone?"

The congressman behind the wheel shrugged his shoulders. "Probably makes him feel like part of the game."

They parked in the circular driveway. As they got out of the car, the younger man noticed a large vehicle sitting in the darkness parked off to the right on the plain grass. It was bigger than a car and had an enormous canvas over it, like a piece of military equipment. "What's that?"

The congressman was dismissive. "Who knows? Rich people have their playthings."

The house itself was sumptuous and set back among parkland in the exclusive and wooded Rock Creek area of Washington. They were shown into a sunken living room which housed a full, nine-foot, concert Steinway, then into an adjoining room with chartreuse walls filled with photographs and framed news articles. They were a montage of Harry's life. On a large Chippendale table were several awards mounted on stands. "This is the trophy room," Harry exclaimed.

He showed them into a dimly lit dining room with a table adorned with candles, fine china, and, finally, a rack of lamb. Harry did most of the talking through dinner, reminiscing about his life and telling anecdotes about the president. Then, after dinner, the men unbuttoned their coats.

Congressman Bromide looked at his snifter of Cognac. "Harry, my friend, we have some vital information for you." He nodded toward his chief of staff.

"Mr. Cone," the younger man said. "You should know that Mark Leduk is pursuing things which are deleterious to the national interest and to the agency. Also, he is bent on destroying you personally. If you don't act on this information, we will have to bring it up before the House Foreign Affairs Committee."

Harry was thunderstruck. He looked at the two men, then at the bottle of fine wine on the table, then at the two men again.

"Pearl Harbor!" he muttered.

Jason and Marilyn were finally able to choose a secretary and program coordinator. They interviewed countless applicants, never having done such a thing before. Then Jason wrote job descriptions establishing what was to be expected of them. The new staff couldn't fit into Clark Kreig's suite of offices, so they were moved to an abandoned ladies apparel shop downstairs at street level. Offices were carved out for each person except the secretary, whose desk sat outside Jason's office. Everything was provided for them: all the latest computer equipment, printers, a fax machine, file cabinets, and a lounge area for visitors. Security even built a separate entrance apart from the main building. Then they put special screens on the floor-length windows, so they could not be penetrated by cameras. They were two-way, so one could see out but no one could see in.

Jason thought that was overkill. Who would want to harm a music program anyway? *Maybe a critic*. He was amused by that thought. But at least there was a lot more room down here. Jason was now an office director with a full staff. He celebrated by buying a bottle of champagne for the office.

Everyone was toasting their new situation when the phone lines lit up. "It's the director of the southern hemisphere area," his secretary told him,

Jason turned on his new speakerphone.

"Brazil," said the voice coming through the box. "Did you hear me? Brazil!"

"Brazil?"

"Yes. Brazil is where you have to send one of these musicians. It is very important right now to our national interest. They should stay down there a month before they go to any other of those countries in South America. And they should go into the provinces, 'chicken-farm' conservatories and teach kids. That'll bring a lot of cachet."

"Sounds good!"

"Glad you agree, Jason, because you're on a high wire. I'll give it to you straight; if this piano player gets a good evaluation cable from the Brazilian embassy down there, it'll put your program into orbit. Nobody will be able to get rid of it. But if the evaluation is lousy... *hasta la vista!*"

Jason gulped his champagne and hung up the phone. The guy was probably right. The evaluation cables would determine everything, and it was the one part of the program he couldn't control: the artists themselves. He didn't know them that well. What were they really like? Would they say or do something untoward, a throwaway comment or some kind of gaffe? Just one bad critical review in the papers could put it all away. It was so volatile. He poured another glass of champagne. The phones lit up again. Jason's secretary moved her swivel chair back to get her legs out from under the desk as quickly as possible. She punched the hold button sharply.

"It's Mr. Cone!"

Jason put the speakerphone on again.

"Please hold for Director Cone."

There was a silence of about six seconds, during which Jason noticed the expectant faces of his staff, all three of them crowding into the doorway. He thought the lineup resembled a shooting gallery. Suddenly, a voice burst through the wire with a rush of words that ran into each other.

"One, two, three, four…"

"Five," said Jason.

"Whaddya mean, five! There's no fifth finger in a chromatic scale, is there?"

"Sorry, I thought you were just counting, and five comes after four." Jason was ready for anything.

"Do you realize that this is the boss of the chiefs? The highest of the high. Of course I know how to count. What I want is the fingering for a chromatic scale."

"The answer is one, two, three, four; one, two, three; one, two, three, four, one."

"Wait a minute, you sound like a computer that's gone berserk."

"But that's the conventional fingering for the chromatic scale beginning on C. Of course there are others."

"See, I need to know all this stuff! Why don't you come up here and show me, but don't advertise it. We're supposed to be doing the people's business."

Jason left the office through the security door facing the courtyard in the rear of the building. He walked outside and turned left toward the back entrance of the main agency. The sunshine felt good—just that little bit of fresh air—before he plunged back into the grey, buzzing fluorescence. He thought about Harry. He had avoided giving him piano lessons, even though the hints had been there. Now that he was in the government, it bothered him to be known as Harry Cone's piano teacher. He also figured that by not giving Harry lessons, it helped make him indispensable. If he continued to dangle the possibility, it would help his survival; Harry would have to keep him around to eventually fulfill the promise. Today was not really going to be a lesson anyway.

As he exited the elevator on the eighth floor, he noticed a coterie of people—maybe three or four in a huddle outside the door leading to Harry's suite of offices. This was routine, people comparing notes before their meeting or maybe even giving each other the courage to go in. He wished he didn't have to go in, especially about this.

"Jason!"

The voice came from behind. He turned and saw Shelley Fatchawada.

She walked up to him and whispered, "Have you heard about Mark Leduk? He's gone!"

"Hadn't noticed."

"It was the die-rek-ta who did it." Her eyes sparkled. "God bless him! He's protecting us, Jason." She pumped her right arm into the air. "He got the president to nominate Leduk to be ambassador to Mugwa."

"Where's that?"

"It's an island off the west coast of Africa."

"That sounds okay."

"Are you nuts? He's been neutered, pushed out of the loop, kicked upstairs into the electric chair. He can't hurt us anymore." She clapped her pudgy hands. "Now, that son of a bitch won't even have an indoor toilet. His wife won't be able to find another trinket for her charm bracelet either. That's justice!" She pumped her arm again, then frowned. "Say, what are you doing up here?"

"Going in to see Harry."

"I'm the one with the appointment," she gasped. "His office said he has to see me. It's very important." She turned and trotted down the long corridor toward Harry's office as her sizable posterior sashayed to some inaudible rhythm.

Jason followed behind her. The top part of her squat trunk, including her head, protruded over her breasts, making her walk not unlike a chicken.

As she came upon the closed door to Harry's office, one of the secretaries said, "Hello."

She turned to acknowledge and banged into the door. Someone opened it from the inside.

The secretary whispered to Jason, "You might as well go in too; it looks like open house today."

He ducked in, trying to be unobtrusive by moving to a spot in the corner against the wall. Shelley was still standing in the doorway in a brightly patterned, flower-bedecked shawl, a loud print dress, elephantine earrings, and a notepad and pencil. Facing her in a semicircle were men of serious mien. Harry Cone sat in the middle like a lion surrounded by cubs dependent on him for sustenance in their daily jungle.

Bill Barron spoke first. He tried to absorb and project the feeling in the room—the director's feeling. His right lip curled slightly, and he said in a snarl, "The director's got a problem!"

All the men stared at Shelley Fatchawada. She felt her heart skip and her life force begin to drain.

"And he wants you to help," said Barron.

Color came back into Shelley's face as quickly as it had left, making her resemble a kaleidoscope.

Harry Cone turned furiously toward his executive assistant. "Last time I looked, I could talk for myself."

Bill Barron absorbed the mixed metaphor by fluttering his eyes, though his face betrayed no sign of emotion. He rose to close the door.

The cold and professional voice of Nate Hinchmin intervened. "Shelley, we are expecting considerable problems both politically and in the media because of a recent occurrence. I believe you are acquainted with the agency's lawyer, Mr. Ogerthorpe. I'll let him explain further."

George Ogerthorpe had been sitting on the couch because he couldn't fit into the smaller armchairs in Harry's office. That's why he always arrived early for meetings, to select an adequate resting place. George liked the couch because, even though he was a mountainous man, he felt he could sink into the cushions with an impassivity that would somehow cause him to be overlooked. But this time he was obliged to speak. His mind searched in a swirl for some neutral ground to lead off. "The director has been accused—"

"Not accused," shouted Harry. "Alleged. Don't my own damn lawyers know the difference?"

"The director is alleged…" George spoke slower now, trying to think through each syllable. This gave him the curious effect of being authoritative while also guarding against slurred words—the by-product of a full bottle of Pinot Noir for lunch. "…is alleged to have installed security devices at his private home at the taxpayers' expense. This includes surveillance cameras, an invisible fence, a round-the-clock private security detail, dogs, flood lights, sirens and…" At this point George's voice began to trail off. "A tank."

Harry exploded. "What do you mean a tank? It's a small armored truck."

George lost his confidence but kept going. "And so,

Ms. Fatchawada, we're all helpless, pardon me, hopeful that the special private get-together committees which you head might be able to cushion..." George sank further into the couch. "...to cushion the negative perceptions in terms of pubic, pardon me, public relations."

Harry stared at George Ogerthorpe, then his eyes swept the rest of the room. "Look at the turkeys I have to work with!"

Shelley laughed because it might please the director, until she remembered she was part of the group referred to.

Bill Barron picked up on the conversation. "Shelley, perhaps you could contact some of the more distinguished people on the committees, those in the private sector, for advice on—"

Harry's rage was uncontrollable. He whipped off his glasses with the speed of a gunslinger reaching for his holster and hurled them across the room. Everyone sat bolt upright. "The more distinguished people on the committee? Hell, they're all distinguished. They're friends of mine!"

Bill Barron was on his hands and knees, looking for Harry's glasses.

"Who in the hell is going to decide who is more distinguished than the other?" Harry shouted. "Certainly not the Foreign Service. They couldn't hold a job in the real world if their lives depended on it." He fastened his gaze on Shelley. "Bring all the committees into Washington. I don't care how you do it, just do it."

Shelley's voice trembled. "Can we pay for it, or do they have to come on their own?"

This was a legal question, so Harry looked at George Ogerthorpe.

George's yellowish eyes moved slowly, like two prehistoric turtles across the great expanse of his face. "We can only pay their way if they don't come." He waited for some reaction, but there was none. The heat in the room was intensifying his discomfort and his condition. "We can offer to pay, but it is imperative they not accept. In this way, the director is blameless before the press and the public. It is the responsibility of Ms. Fatchawada to finesse this point with the committees and get them to agree to commit their own resources for the journey."

The effects of that bottle of wine were wearing off. George sensed the dangerous zone of sobriety that he was entering. He needed something strong, not artsy-craftsy but straight up.

Meanwhile, Shelley Fatchawada was contemplating the task laid before her: trying to get Harry Cone's friends to pay for their own trip to Washington to bail him out of trouble. Thoughts raced across her mind. She had gravitated toward power for as long as she could remember. But now, for the first time, she found appealing something she had previously found appalling: being a librarian somewhere far away.

Jason stood against the wall next to the door. As Shelley left, she opened the door blocking him from Harry's view. When she closed it, Harry finally noticed him.

"What are you doing here?"

The others looked at Jason.

"One... two, three, four," he stammered.

"Oh, yeah." The director motioned for Jason to follow him. They went into Harry's private bathroom where the director shut the door and quickly flushed the toilet.

"Okay, what is it," he said in a hushed voice.

Jason froze. "The chromatic scale," he whispered.

"Well, show me." Harry closed the lid of the commode, and Jason demonstrated on top of it.

"The thumb passes under that often?"

"Yes."

Harry turned abruptly and opened the door. He and Jason walked out while the men still waiting in the room looked at them peculiarly. Jason avoided eye contact as he headed for the exit and the elevators. He pushed the down button and tried to collect himself. He had come a long way in a short time. He had learned to adapt to the political atmosphere and the endless details of the bureaucracy and the danger zones that followed him everywhere. But it was the irrationality that stayed with him, the lunacy. That, he couldn't shake. Why had

Harry taken him out of his office and into the adjoining bathroom, flushed the toilet, and started whispering? Between floors, someone asked him if it was still sunny out. He replied he didn't know and realized he was still whispering.

The next morning while sipping coffee in his office, he saw both Marilyn and his secretary running across the courtyard toward his office. The security system beeped, and the door slammed.

Marilyn came in out of breath. "Big time scandal!" she said, throwing the morning edition of the *Washington Post* down on his desk.

"I already know about it," he said. "Harry had some security stuff installed and—"

"No, Jason, that's on page twelve. Look what's on the front page."

Jason unfolded the paper.

WASHINGTON, DC - Harold Cone, the bumptious director of the International Cultural Communications Agency and the president's "closest friend," has been accused of secretly tape recording conversations in his office. The alleged list of people who have been taped, including phone conversations, carries the names of some of Washington's biggest political celebrities. Perhaps even the president of the United States. Critics of Mr. Cone are comparing him to a dictator, and others are accusing him of being a throwback to the days of Watergate. Still, others are asking, "When will he go?"

Jason looked up. "So that's why he took me into the bathroom."

"What?" said Marilyn.

"He didn't want that mini piano lesson on tape, so he took me into his private bathroom. That must be the only place he's not taping."

Marilyn grimaced. "I'm so glad he has the good judgment not to tape in the bathroom."

The limousine moved smoothly over the cold, black-tar, circular driveway. Everything was surgically clean, even the freshly painted columns on the North Portico of the executive mansion. As the car came to a halt, Harry sprang from the back seat almost simultaneously as a marine guard opened the door. He ran up the red-carpeted steps and through the entrance. As he walked the corridors, it was quiet. Only the rustle of clothing betrayed people inside who walked about with abnormal intensity. Harry walked up to the door of the Oval Office. A marine guard saluted. Harry was always amused by that. He had never performed military service, but if you had power, he reasoned, that was a shortcut.

He entered quickly through the doorway. The president was sitting on a colorful sofa in the center of the room. Harry spoke in a loud voice. "A man crossed a tiger with a parakeet. He didn't know what he got, but when it talked, he listened."

The president laughed. "Harry, I was just wondering whether or not France is in NATO. Is it?"

"Gee, I thought it was in Europe."

Both men laughed.

"By the way, what are we gonna do to get the housing industry on its feet?" Now Harry looked serious. "People can't afford homes."

"I don't know, Harry. What do you think?"

"First, we oughta get the secretary of housing on his feet. I saw him at a party last night, and he could barely walk."

The president's shoulders shook. He laughed with his upper torso jingling like a puppet on a string.

"Hell, everything's a problem in this town." Harry looked vexed. "Look at me! The press is chewing me up."

The president stood. "Don't worry. I'll call the chairman of the investigating committee and tell him to go easy. And someone on my wife's staff will call the *Washington Post*. They'll lay off, too."

Harry felt every tissue in his body suddenly begin to regenerate—the certain sign of a long and peaceful life.

"Now, Harry, have you got another one?"

"Another what?"

"Joke."

Harry double blinked, his eyes darting. "Uh… A fat man went for a physical. The doctor said, 'Your weight is perfect. Only problem is you're eleven feet too short.'"

He got into his limousine and saw the driver had already removed the dummy keyboard from the trunk. Putting it on his lap seemed so natural. His fingers started meandering over the keys before the car even got out of the gate. Every muscle in his body was uncontracted and supple—like a cat asleep. Once more, he had gotten what he wanted. To think the *Washington Post* and Congress would leave him alone… That was the greatest tranquilizing agent he could ingest.

It was early evening, and the moon was already out. Harry stared out the window, trying to imagine how many great men had been inspired by it. Then, his fingers fell into the pattern of the song, "Moon Over Miami." The car phone rang. Harry was irritated at being taken out of his reverie. It was Bill Barron.

"I caught the head of the Office of Press Relations in a lie today. And he's been aggravating a couple people on his staff too. I just thought you should know, Mr. Director."

"Get rid of him," said Harry.

"Well, what we could do, what we've done in other situations, is to put him on a consultancy for a while to tide him over until he finds—"

"I don't want to tide him over," barked the director. "I want the tide to take him out to sea!"

He slammed the phone down and let his head rest on the back of the seat to clear his mind. It took a moment. Then, softly, as if from a distance, he began to croon the lyrics to "Moon Over Miami;" then he switched to "Harvest Moon;" then he remembered a song from his youth. Even more quietly now, and from the recess of his memory, he began the chorus in an almost inaudible whisper. "There's a place in France, where the women wear no pants…" Suddenly, he looked around startled, as if there might be someone else in the back seat. *Boy, that wouldn't go over*, he thought. Maybe he ought to learn some of the new stuff. Harry knew he had a generational problem and needed to be around younger people. Also, he needed to improve his rendition of "Moon Over Miami." He had to convince Jason Angeletti to give him piano lessons.

The weather turned cold. There was an early snowfall, and it wasn't even Christmas. That was the elevator talk, anyway, when people had nothing else to say between floors: "Very unusual in Washington, a snowfall in November... Wonder what it means."

Things had to mean something. That was a way of deciphering what would come next in the dizzying atmospherics of Washington. Life in the modern Rome of western civilization was like the proportion of a canine's life to a human: seven years compressed into one.

Jason thought how quickly time had passed. Yesterday, he was in trouble, today Harry Cone. Harry got off easy in his appearance before a congressional investigating committee, but some suggested he might face indictment in the court system. Jason, however, was growing stronger daily within the agency. He was even greeted randomly by people he did not know—a sure sign of celebrity.

He had already sent out cables to American embassies throughout the world offering the Musical Emissary Program, and there were plenty of takers. The embassies now felt the three-stage selection process of the program plus the low cost were reasons enough to take a chance, so the tours were lining up with each of the two pianists covering six different countries over eight weeks. Jason wanted the artists brought to Washington to be briefed by Foreign Service Officers who handled those countries for the agency. Neville Yamamoto Bettelheim would be the first since he was going to Brazil. There was a large population of Japanese in the cities of Recife and São Paulo, and since Neville's appearance was more oriental than European or Semitic, it seemed good public relations. Jason had to find out who the desk officer was for Brazil.

Jack Chinook wondered when he would get sent back overseas. He had been on duty in Germany for years, before the agency decided to rotate him for paperwork in Washington. He even brought back a German wife. Now the excitement had ended. No more cooks or household staff, no perks, whatever —just a townhouse in Alexandria, Virginia. He even had to mow the lawn over the weekend. His new job as desk officer for Brazil was no big deal. All outgoing and incoming cables to that post had to go through him. That was all. But if he wanted to go back overseas, he had to do a good job. His evaluation report was due, and it would be written by a former underling who now outranked him. He racked his brain, wondering if he had ever screwed this guy. In the Foreign Service, it was called the boomerang effect when someone came around later to get back at you. *Be nice to everybody on the way up*, he thought, *because you'll meet them again coming down.*

Jason Angeletti walked into the reasonably large office befitting Jack Chinook's rank and number of years in service. He saw a coatless, middle-aged man with his feet up on the desk and the swivel chair tipped back. His red suspenders and blue shirt clashed with a tie that featured the green and yellow colors of the Brazilian flag. There was a small replica of the

Christ the Redeemer statue from Rio de Janeiro on his desk and a painting of the Amazon River on the wall. A single window provided a view of a railroad track and parking lots.

Jason pointed to the painting on the wall. "Must be nice."

"What?"

"Brazil."

Jack shrugged his shoulders. "Dunno, I've never been there."

"But you're the resident expert."

"Hey, I read what they give me. Anyway, I'm going there for a conference next month. It'll be good to get the hell out of here and away from that crazy director we've got."

"Have you had a run-in?"

"Just what I read in the papers. The guy has embarrassed the agency and the meaning of diplomacy. He's been secretly taping in his office. Nobody knows what's on those tapes or who he's recorded. I've never seen morale so low in the agency. It's dangerously low. Call it the herd mentality or lack of leadership, but when the head falls, the body follows. People can't stand this guy. I talked to the head of the printing office today, and he's ready to jump out the window. Except his office is on the ground floor."

The next day a cold, damp wind swept through Washington, heralding the first week of December. It reminded him of the end of the winter semester at East Chalmers University. Could it already be the second year he had been here? He looked through the two-way window in his office. People outside walked by in overcoats and scarves, rubbing their hands to keep warm. When they stopped to talk to someone, their breath was visible, like a cloud vapor. He felt a sense of well-being in the warmth of the office; it felt cozy.

He had settled nicely into a routine. The program was being put together incrementally. Jason always liked goals to be set and then to achieve them in steps. It was the only way to put together a concert program and, apparently, to administrate. In the evenings, he practiced on his small grand and then had dinner. To keep up the piano meant a close scheduling in his life. He had chosen his little basement apartment because its location was only one metro stop from the agency. That meant more time to practice, but everything else was convenient as well: the drycleaners, a small grocery store, and restaurants. Marilyn stayed with him on the weekends, and they planned outings every Sunday. His life seemed in balance.

On this morning, she came into his office suggesting they work on a travel grant for Neville Yamamoto Bettelheim's briefing in Washington. Jason countered with plans for the two of them that weekend when the siren went off. It was startling at first. There was a brief pause. Then it began wailing continuously. Everyone moved for their coats and the security door, exiting into the courtyard. Then the secretary and program coordinator broke into a run for the doors of the main agency. They headed for the lobby and the main avenue of escape, the entrance onto Seventh Street. It was already crowded.

"A bomb scare," people muttered, making their way out of the building.

Upstairs, the office directors were mobilizing their staffs into an orderly withdrawal, but most employees did not wait. Clark Kreig, the director of the Office of Personal Exchange, walked from one partition to the other, looking for employees under his aegis. He wore the obligatory defense helmet designed for evacuations. Under the duress, his facial tics made the unbuttoned straps on the side of the helmet flap against the hard plastic. The regularity was metronomic as he searched for people, most of whom had already gone.

Downstairs, two different security guards, each with electronic megaphones, gave conflicting instructions. One ordered people already outside to come back in because it was a false alarm. The other urged them to cross the street to safety. Droves of humanity who were trying to get out collided with those trying to get back in.

Men stood on the street with heavy parkas over their suits. Some women, in the rush, carried out whatever they had been holding inside—paper, reports, or file folders. Jason walked into the crowd chatting until someone called his name… and then another. Suddenly, it was being whispered everywhere. He looked around.

A voice broke above the throng. "Jason, it's the director!"

The crowd parted into two halves, making a human path toward a black limousine. The car rested imposingly at the curbside like an impregnable citadel. The dark, bulletproof window in the back seat was half rolled down like a draw-bridge while an anonymous arm beckoned from the window. The limb was bedecked in French cuffs and presidential cuff links that glistened in the morning sun.

As Jason walked down the human corridor, it reminded him of a military wedding. As he drew nearer, the back window rolled down farther. Harry's shadowy face emerged, a study in darkness.

"I don't deserve this shit!"

"What's going on?"

"They're trying to blow the place up."

Jason looked at the building nonchalantly. "Well, so far, they haven't succeeded." He wondered if his optimism was tempting providence.

Harry decided not to look at the building. "Jason, I should congratulate you on your accomplishments, on what you have done and will continue to do. And I want you to take all the good news and put it in a book, a very big book. Then we're gonna take it to all those people who said I put you on the payroll because we're friends, and we'll shove it up their ass."

As if on cue, Harry receded into the back seat as the black window rolled up like a curtain descending on the last act of a play. The car moved slowly into traffic, and Jason started back toward the building. Noises in the gallery formed the word "access." Someone said clearly, "He really is a friend of Harry Cone!"

Shortly after the New Year, Neville Yamamoto Bettelheim arrived in Washington for his briefings with the Foreign Service. He was quiet and attentive with a constant, faint smile. The smile never left, no matter what the content of the conversation or situation was. He took notes and asked a few questions, but there was not much information in the briefings that was of any value. He had one press interview, and the resulting article, which appeared over the weekend, impressed the bureaucrats. The trip appeared to be a success. Still, Jason gave the musical emissary his own personal "briefing." On Neville's last night in Washington, Jason invited him to dinner at his own expense. They dined at a small Chinese restaurant on H Street.

"Neville, you realize these will not be ordinary concerts overseas. You won't be playing for your own self-aggrandizement; you will be representing the United States of America. The way you walk and talk and the things you say will be analyzed and considered as examples of American culture. In fact, everyone will be told that you're the very best we can send overseas for others to judge us by."

"I understand. It's a great honor indeed," said Neville, with a slightly clipped British accent.

Jason smiled at the irony. Here was an American citizen who was part Jewish, English, and Japanese, nominated by the San Francisco Conservatory of Music despite living in England. It was too multicultural to be true.

Neville read his mind. "Jason, did you ever wonder why I like to live in England?"

"No, why?"

"Because over there you can wear a dress and makeup and nobody cares."

Jason stared as though dumbstruck. He shivered as he imagined Neville walking on stage in a strapless gown. Neither did it escape him that Neville had a beard. Like a drowning man, his whole life flashed before his eyes.

He went home and placed a late-night call to the Catholic monk. He couldn't get through, but the priest he spoke to gave him a message from Father O'Malley. "Nothing can be done at this point, Jason, except hope and prayer."

The next day, the agency magazine released a cover story on

the auditions. It included an interview with Harry Cone where he praised the selection process of the Musical Emissary Program as being "grassroots and foolproof."

Marilyn and Jason walked through the palatial rooms, studying each painting. He loved the French Impressionist collection in the West Wing of the National Gallery, preferring things like that to receptions, cocktail parties, and the embassy circuit. Marilyn had already given all that up to be with him. The weekends were something they both looked forward to, and it was a brilliant, sunny Sunday. He pointed to the vivid colors that Renoir and Monet achieved by not blending the oils, how color was more important to them than line and how free bush strokes were used in the natural open air.

She drank it in and held his hand, until they came to the *Boulevard des Italiens* by Pissarro. "That's a little different from the others." Marilyn was learning and checking her instincts.

"Pointillism," he said, enjoying the moment. "Everything's put together with tiny pinpoint… little dots which allow the eye to move out into a larger scheme."

They took a break and went downstairs to the café for a drink of chilled white wine. It was the pale shank of the afternoon, and they sat by the waterfall.

She gazed at him, with pleasure. But she had also become preternaturally sensitive to his moods. "What's wrong, Jason?"

He looked surprised. "It's Neville."

"Why? Because he's gay?"

"No, because he wears dresses, has a beard, and goes on stage. There's a lot at stake, Marilyn. This Washington thing is like a merry-go–round. Just when you think you've got it going, something comes at you."

"He's not going to do anything stupid when he's down there. He's an intelligent person and knows what's expected of him."

"You sound like you really know him. I don't."

"It's just common sense. Cheer up! Things are even looking up for Mr. Cone. It looks like there won't be an indictment for the taping, and even the papers have dropped it."

"That's because Harry Cone never wore a dress on stage."

"You're obsessing." Marilyn looked at her watch and suggested they leave for an early film in Georgetown.

They walked down three flights of the great staircase to the main lobby and exited out the Fourth Street entrance toward the car. They usually took cabs in Washington, but this time, Marilyn wanted to drive. He didn't know why. There was never any place to park in Georgetown.

They maneuvered traffic until they were safely on M Street

going into the heart of the Northwest quadrant of the District of Columbia along the Potomac waterfront. Georgetown was lively on the weekend. Well-dressed people, casual and mostly young, were rushing past the high-end shops and exotic stores. Some were coming out of small art galleries deep in discussion, or heading into boutique restaurants. As a fashion and cultural center, bookstores tempted people with blown-up covers of best sellers smacked against the window front.

Marilyn zoomed past all of it, including the intersection at Wisconsin Avenue where the movie theater was. She kept driving down M Street until it merged into Canal Road and into Foxhall, one of the most affluent neighborhoods in Washington.

Jason knew something was strange. "What are you doing? We missed the turnoff!"

"It's a surprise, darling."

Tudor houses reeled by, one after the other, dazzling in opulence and set back amongst the oak and shrubbery. She turned into a driveway and drove through an open gate, then parked the car under the portico of a mansion.

Jason looked up at the massive chimney, the overlapping gables, and broad embankments. A manservant answered the doorbell and showed them into a large foyer. A staircase bordered one side and louvre doors led into adjoining rooms. One of them, a library, had bookshelves stretching the circumference of the room and up to the ceiling. A ladder stood prominently along one wall, with a marble table dominating the center of the room. A clock encased in gold chimed the hour. But the stillness was broken by a cry.

"Wendell!" shouted Jason.

Wendell Marchant was seated in front of the fireplace. He tried to assemble his large frame in order to get out of the armchair. With a Cheshire cat grin, he gave a courtly bow to Marilyn and a nod to Jason. His bald dome shined even in the soft light.

"What are you doing here, old friend?" Jason was perplexed.

"I was invited and gladly agreed to upgrade my existence for an hour or so."

Jason looked at Marilyn.

Two doors with moveable slats unexpectedly opened. A tall, distinguished man with pure-white hair and an aquiline nose entered the room. His suit was immaculately tailored to his spare frame, and his tie had a Picasso-like design of abstract figures.

"You must be Jason Angeletti!" He extended his hand. "I have become a great admirer of yours. I had the privilege of attending your auditions at the Library of Congress one charming afternoon, and left in awe of what you've accomplished with our government. My name is Stephan Wopplebanger."

"Nice to meet you." Jason had to play it out.

"Would anyone like refreshments?" Stephan picked up a little bell and rang it.

The manservant came back in with a tray of sugar cookies and glasses of dry sherry that he set on the table.

"Please help yourselves while I come to the point." He nodded in Marilyn's direction. "This lovely lady arranged the meeting today through my old friend, Wendell Marchant. They both believe in you, Jason. And I have joined them. I know this town and what can happen, and I want to help ensure that your program survives. They have convinced me that by show-casing your own talent, the Musical Emissary Program will be enhanced. After all, how many people in Washington can actu-ally do what they administrate? So I have agreed to sponsor you in a Kennedy Center recital."

Jason's face lit up.

Stephan looked at Wendell. "You've heard him play, right?"

"Yup. On the road during the auditions. We got to a hall early once, and he tried the piano. Wound up playing a number of things for me. I was impressed. Jason could have a major career as a performer if the chips fell in the right place."

Stephan smiled. "There you have it. And from one of the best critics in the country. I'll put up the money to rent the hall, pay for tickets, and whatever else, but I don't want any publicity. My guess is that I'll get my investment back because the hall will be filled with your colleagues. All the bureaucrats will be curious if you can really play." He looked again at Wendell. "When should this be scheduled?"

"After the first evaluation cables start coming in on these artists. My guess is they'll be full of unstinted praise. Then the concert will be like a one-two punch."

Stephan nodded. "By the way, is anybody going to Brazil? I have some business ventures down there."

Jason turned white. Wendell noticed something was wrong.

"Yes, we... eh..." Jason couldn't put any words together.

Stephan shot a question. "Is there a problem?"

Marilyn spoke up. "It's just that Jason isn't entirely sure about one of the artists, the one chosen for Brazil."

"What's wrong with him?"

Deafening silence.

"Come now," said Stephan insistently. "If I'm going to be of help to your program I might as well start now."

Marilyn was nervous. "It's just that this particular artist is very sensitive and—"

"He's a cross dresser," Jason blurted out. "He wears dresses."

Wendell's eyes narrowed. "Which one is it?"

"Neville Yamamoto..."

"Oh hell, I heard him play on the road. He's so good; nobody will care. Besides, some people in the embassy down there might be just like him. You never know. They'll know how to handle it."

Stephan looked amused. "I want you all to meet someone."

He opened one of the slats in the door. "Helmut?"

A slight man emerged with thinning hair, wearing a velour jacket and an ascot. "I am so happy to meet all of you," he said with a light, cosmopolitan accent. "My name is Helmut Roseleip, and you are all to be congratulated for what you have accomplished. I too was at your auditions, and the American government should be doing more things like this." He circled the room with grace and shook everyone's hand.

Stephan watched with a kind eye. "Helmut and I are life partners," he said. "We have been together for thirty years, and he has given meaning to my life."

Marilyn smiled without missing a beat. "Congratulations!"

Wendell shook his head. "Thirty years? You can't say that's not love."

Then everyone looked at Jason; this was outside his realm. He felt like Custer at Little Bighorn, the last one standing.

Princess Little Feather Susquat was the older of the two

musical emissaries. She was forty-six years old and tall, with long black hair and an elongated face that resembled a portrait by El Greco. Lanky and ungainly, she walked like a tall reed that bent in different places. Now a part-time typist from the Midwest, she had had a promising start as a child prodigy before abandoning the piano as part of some spiritual quest. "You can't hear yourself when you're always making noise," she told a puzzled reporter for the *Chicago Tribune*. Now, she had come out of retirement for the Musical Emissary Program. Her Cherokee background made for good copy, and the Office of Press Relations landed her several press interviews while she was at the agency for her briefings with the Caribbean desk officers.

She asked several questions in those briefings which did not seem pertinent. One had to do with suntan lotion. "It's hot down there, isn't it?" Another, concerned poor people. "We should just hand out cash from the stage. That would make everybody look good." Her laugh was incessant and, in the higher registers, somewhat grating.

Jason wondered if the Foreign Service interviewers had picked up on any of this. But most things went smoothly and uneventfully, until she and Jason went down to the lobby on their way to lunch.

Harry Cone saw them across the expanse of the building and left his entourage to come over. Jason introduced Princess Little Feather, and she seized the initiative before anything else could be said.

193

"Mr. Cone, has anybody ever told you that you look just like Richard Nixon? Now, he may have been a disgraced president," she added, moving closer, "but he was president... if you know what I mean." She punctuated her remarks with a falsetto giggle.

"I've been disgraced, but I've never been president." Harry offered a toothy smile.

"We'd better be going," said Jason, nervously.

"I usually tell Jason when he can go and, occasionally, where he can go." Harry's smile turned into a leer.

Little Feather jumped in. "You know, Mr. Cone, the more I look at you, the more I just think that all of you look alike... you know, the political types." She giggled in a high pitch that sounded like a flute. "It's like going into a bank and looking at all those photos of past bank presidents. I can't tell one from the other."

Harry took Jason aside. "Who in the hell is that anyway?"

"That's a musical emissary." Jason could hear his heart pound. He squeezed the words out.

Harry frowned. "I thought this program was for young people, but this woman has got to be pushing fifty!"

Jason felt danger. "Art should have no age limit," he stammered. "She needs a chance, too."

Harry thumped his chest. "If I'd have known that, I might have auditioned myself."

Jason felt the earth move.

Then Harry smiled. "Only kidding," he said.

Princess Little Feather's briefings took Jason's mind off Neville's trip. Neville had begun his grand odyssey days before, but Jason had barely thought about it. He filled his time instead ushering Little Feather from one desk officer to another in the agency. But now that it was over, and she was gone, he was alone with his thoughts. One cable had already come in about Neville, but it said only that he had arrived and was resting from the multiple vaccinations he had taken before leaving. It was days later that Marilyn stuck her head in the office.

"A heads-up call from Brazil for you, Jason."

"What's a heads-up call?"

She rolled her eyes toward the ceiling. "Darling, you've got to learn these things. It's an unofficial call from an embassy employee. The purpose is to alert you to a problem without actually going on the record."

Jason heard the word "problem" and stared at the phone. "I told you so!"

Marilyn rolled her eyes again.

"Mr. Angeletti?" said the voice on the wire.

"Yes."

"Thank you for sending us such a brilliant talent."

"You're welcome."

"We don't often get artists of this caliber down here."

"Perhaps not."

"He has incredible technique and interpretive depth."

"We thought so."

"And what an example of American cultural pluralism.

"Right."

"And everything is so incredibly vivid about the man."

"How's that?"

"Not only his projection of emotion and musical ideas but also his powerful physical appearance on the stage."

Jason's mind was clicking. Neville Yamamoto Bettleheim was only five feet and four inches tall. "What's so vivid and powerful about his physical presence?"

"Well, the lights and darks of his countenance. They almost seem to go with the ebb and flow and mood of the music he's playing."

"Could you describe his countenance?"

"His face is very pale, his eyes are dark and ruminative, and his lips are robust and red."

"He's wearing makeup?"

"Well, when the foreign minister embraced him after the concert, he wound up with lipstick on his cheek."

"He isn't—" The words wouldn't come. "He isn't wearing a dress, is he?"

"No, but it's unseasonably cold here right now, and he's wearing a floor-length fox coat, which is a little borderline, I guess."

Jason tracked Neville down in the small town of Aracaju on the northeast coast of Brazil. The American embassy alerted the hotel staff to the call, and Neville waited in his room.

"Neville, you're doing a great job down there, but I want you to cut back on some of the gloss."

"What do you mean?"

"Clean up your act a little."

"Could you be more specific, Jason?"

"Get rid of the lipstick and mascara."

"Can I keep some powder on?"

"Okay. Maybe they'll think you've got a fever."

"Some of them like it, you know."

"What do you mean?"

"Some of the people in the embassy are like me."

It was toward the end of the month that Neville's evaluation cable came in from Brazil. Marilyn was the first to read it. The corners of her lips curled into a half smile as she handed it to Jason. He read it out loud while the secretary looked over his shoulder.

> *WE LOVE THIS MAN! Seldom in the course of history does a great talent blend with the magnificent allure of perfect physical proportions to create the charisma we have just experienced. Moving across the continent with the lithe grace of a gazelle, this handsome, strong man won hearts and minds for America while, at the same time, getting under our skin. We shall miss him terribly, but will never forget that once there was a Camelot.*

Jason reread it. He had never seen a government cable like it. He chided himself on being cynical, but he couldn't help thinking that somewhere, somehow, and with someone, Neville had been a sexual smash.

The phones lit up. The first call was from the area director for the southern hemisphere.

"You did it, kid! Your program's in cement now, and nobody can shake it. That cable from Brazil is the best evaluation cable I've ever read!"

There was pandemonium in the outer office while his secretary whisked in with a brown envelope. "It's from the director's office."

Jason broke the seal carefully.

Dear Jason:

I wanted to take this opportunity to offer my congratulations on the astounding success of your smashing program. A superlative review from a very important country has come to my attention, and it is no less than magical. Through this program, the vibrating sounds of the piano will be heard throughout the world. And nobody will need a hearing aid because the sounds will bypass the ears and go directly to the heart. You have made a gift to the world of music, just as if you tied a ribbon around the piano and allowed people to take it home in their pocket.

Sincerely,
Harold Cone
Director

He tested the ink. It would not come off the signature when he wetted it, so he figured it was stamped. But it sure sounded like Harry.

Marilyn drove him by the dry cleaners on the way home that night so he could pick up his tuxedo. When he got into his apartment, he threw everything down on the bed and went to the piano, as he had done every night. Four hours later, he finished practicing. *I've got to be ready*, he told himself. Things were happening fast.

He stood in the wings shaking. This was the moment he had wanted and waited for, the big time, the Kennedy Center. Now he was scared. *How many out there*, he wondered? Quite a few to make that undercurrent of noise. He went through his litany of fears: Would there be any critics? Was his fly closed? Would he embarrass himself? And what about a memory slip?

The house lights dimmed, and the murmuring of the crowd stopped. He started the long walk across the stage of the Kennedy Center Terrace Theater to the piano. He felt strangely small and shriveled. *Don't judge me too harshly*, he wanted to say. The applause sounded considerable. He reached the piano, turned front and center, and bowed. He noticed in the flash of an instant, a large contingency of political appointees sitting in tuxedos and evening dresses, on the left side of the auditorium. On the right side were career people, dressed more casually. *My God*, he thought, *even my concert is politically polarized.* As he sat down to the piano, he wondered if there were any other people there besides agency employees.

His fingers shook as he started a Scarlatti sonata. *Not to worry*, he thought. *The piece is slow and more easily controllable for this condition.* He had planned it that way. Experience dictated that the nervous shakes would leave about five minutes after he was out there. Unfortunately, the first piece lasted only three minutes. He started the second sonata, which had faster scale passages. His fingers were still shaking, so the passage work was uneven. Then he started the longer Bach partita. He played it softly, afraid the whole thing might fall apart. His fingers should have stopped trembling by now; this was a bad sign. Then, at the end of the piece, they finally did stop.

At last, he was able to take more chances, but it was too late. The piece was over. The applause was polite as he got up to bow and then sat down again. Now, he began the late Beethoven sonata that would close the first half of the program. He started it a little too quickly, but there was momentum. He had become less self-conscious. He played the second movement faster than he thought possible, but it enhanced the music. By the last movement, he was lost in sound, riding a wave of emotion. And when he moved from the backbreaking trills on the last page to the final reprise of the theme, there was a cathedral-like silence in the hall. He spun out the closing chords and left his hands on the keyboard for a moment.

After the sound disappeared, shouts erupted. *Bravo! Bravo!*

There followed an avalanche of applause that seemed to grow each second. He stood and stared, still emotionally caught up in the music, then bowed deeply. He was called back several times, each time walking closer to the edge of the stage. He felt it was safe to move nearer to the audience; his confidence was growing.

After a fifteen-minute intermission, he came back to play the final work on the program, Schumann's *Carnaval*. He tore into the opening dramatic chords and, for thirty minutes, moved through the knotty problems of each small, colorful section with assurance. The music gradually took shape, creating a surge of emotion. The final ear-splitting chords brought the concert to a dizzying end and elicited an overwhelming reception from the left side of the auditorium. An army of tuxedos and gowns rose as one body to give a standing ovation. People on the right side remained seated.

Jason went into the dressing room exhausted.

Marilyn raced in, overcome with tears. She held him for a long moment, then whispered, "Jason, you have no idea how high your star is rising. Just like we planned. You'll be a household word in Washington." She spoke in a soft, nocturnal whisper that aroused him.

They went out and stood together in the receiving line backstage while everyone filed past, expressing congratulations. Many of the career people could not hide their amazement. He stood, resplendent in his tuxedo, feeling part of some triumphal procession. Even Bonita Baracuddle expressed begrudging appreciation.

One woman approached him breathing heavily, her pupils dilated. "You... you..." She trailed off and tried to regroup. "You... should be president of the United States!"

Jason cringed. He would have preferred a comment about his interpretation of the late Beethoven sonata.

Marilyn smiled and squeezed his hand. She had never felt so energized.

Shelley Fatchawada cut in front of the line. "Jason, I'm having a reception for you at my house. It's all set, and I've got somebody to drive you two. Congratulations on a great concert, fella. You made the die-rek-ta look good. But where in the hell is he, anyway? I couldn't find him all night. I guess something came up, but maybe he'll be at the reception."

"I don't think so. I didn't invite him to my concert, so he probably won't be at your house either."

"What?" she shrieked. "Are you nuts? You're really nuts. What are you, *un imbécile?*"

Jason went for the kill. "Look, the director is poison right now, but I'm big."

Shelley's jaw went slack.

The palm trees moved in slow motion, rocking gently in the translucent light of the moon. A breeze off the Caribbean Sea seemed to engulf all living things in its gentle fold. The sweet smell of rum and cherries was locked into frosted glasses that tinkled and clinked as people carried them to their seats after intermission. The new outdoor amphitheater was close to the beach in the open air. The acoustical shell underneath was built with concentric arches, so the sound was full and clear, even amidst the waves lapping off the coastline. The latest technology was used so that the seats could be adjusted, and the lighting system would make everything perfectly clear, even on the darkest of nights. And since the temperature varied little year-round because the tropical trade winds neutralized the heat and humidity, the concert schedule was full throughout the year.

Princess Little Feather Susquat stood in the wings, awaiting the first concert on her musical emissary tour: a performance of Rachmaninoff's Piano Concerto No. 2 with the National Symphony Orchestra of the Dominican Republic. Ostrich feathers sprouted like wings from the shoulders of her white-sequined formal gown. A shoot of eagle feathers climbed up dramatically from behind her head, arrayed in a horizontal pattern resembling an oriental fan. She walked onto the stage with the conductor in tow and began a long, lonely walk to the piano in front of twenty-five hundred people. Her long, spare frame moved in two parts, with the lower torso lagging behind like Ichabod Crane. Her lank face was surrounded by plumes and feathers, which gave the impression that there was little to anchor the center.

"*India Americana,*" people whispered. One person said she looked like a prehistoric bird which had landed in the wrong Ice Age. After fiddling with the concert bench for a moment, she nodded to the conductor. He looked to his troops to begin the great battle of broadswords between the orchestra and the soloist in one of the supreme virtuoso concertos of the Romantic literature. But it was up to her to begin.

She started the long, stretched chords softly, each answered by a low bass note that tolled something ominous. Chords mounted, gaining in fistfuls of notes and intensity until the crashing end brought in the full orchestra. At this point, the audience stopped watching the feathers. They were uniformly caught up in the ardor and Russian passion of the piece. The famous and rather sentimental theme of the first movement was played directly and without affectation, making it even more striking. But there was a wildness in the difficult cadenza passages that held people spellbound. Then the great, thick, full-throated chords that Rachmaninoff wrote for his own enormous hands, four notes in each webbed finger, took over the dictum. The piano shook as Princess Little Feather struck them from high above the keyboard, bouncing like a trapeze artist from the tonic harmonies to the dominant. Her abnormally long arms were levers to her spidery fingers as they came crashing down on the keyboard. The orchestra pursued her, milking her, building the drama block upon block, into a dizzying, orgiastic spiral. Unresolved, the piano continued like a gladiator in the struggle, pushing until the music exploded into a colossal Russian Hopak danced only on Mount Olympus.

Then... the lights went out. Pitch blackness and deafening silence. A collective gasp sounded from the audience. The orchestra stopped playing, one confused section after another in fading cacophony, then finally the soloist. After a moment, chatter started. Cigar smokers took out matchboxes and lit small fires but to no avail. People did not move because vision was limited, but there was shuffling on the stage as the orchestra blindly tried to find its way off.

It seemed like an endless amount of time before, ever so gently, strains of one of the popular themes from the concerto started coming from the gloomy, black hole where the pianist now sat alone. There were wrong notes as Little Feather, unseeing, groped the keyboard, but the tune was recognizable. A man came from the wings with a flashlight. He seized a chair in front of one of the empty orchestra stands and sat down, focusing the light on the keyboard.

Little Feather began again, this time the Sonata No. 2 in B-flat minor of Chopin. She played the first movement like a poem of death, making the hollow loneliness of the empty, dark sky seem even nearer to the listeners. The second movement began like a "Dance Macabre," and by the time the Funeral March began, the portentous feeling was unbearable. When she began the short, last movement, it was wind over the grave, a blur of fast notes rippling by, and then, just as suddenly, it was over.

Applause started slowly and grew until it was tumultuous. Little Feather didn't acknowledge it. No one could see her anyway; only the outline of her hands from the small circle of light. Instead, she launched into the *Waldstein* sonata of Beethoven before the applause even stopped. It was a cheerier piece, less emotional and more like a sunrise. She played with verve and gusto, dispensing easily with its pianistic pratfalls, from fast scales and trills to *tremoli*.

And when that was over, one hour having already gone by, the public, forgetting their plight, asked for more. They stared at the small beam of light on the stage and kept applauding. She began the *Kreisleriana* of Robert Schumann. Waves of passion and turbulence so much a part of Kreisler, the half-mad conductor and composer from German fiction, were wedded to moments of sublime lyricism. The great Romantic masterwork in eight episodes unfolded in Little Feather's hands with pathos and tenderness, baring for all to see the broken soul and inner turmoil of Kreisler's life.

But it was during the finale that something went awry. Jack boots could be heard in the distance. Unrelenting and metronomic, they became louder with each step. Distant voices gave orders to shoot on sight or to inveigh against anything suspicious in the audience.

Paramilitary troops marched from the entrance of the

amphitheater to the stage, walking the aisles back and forth with machine guns pointed upward, looking left and right... left, right. One soldier sent up a flare which climbed into the darkness and exploded overhead with the bark of a firecracker. A woman screamed. Suddenly, the lights went on.

The audience remained silent as the soldiers marched out, their boots making loud clacks on the parquet aisles. Little Feather stood on the stage staring out, her long arms hanging down like boughs of a tree that had been broken. The audience stared back.

The sound of the boots was still in the distance when she seated herself once more at the piano to play the short Prélude of Debussy, *Footsteps in the Snow*. Those who knew the piece began to titter, but when she finished in the softness of a hush, there was graveyard silence.

After a moment, a sole person shouted *"Brava... Americana!"*

People leapt to their feet in unison, yelling and screaming. Pandemonium broke out as the applause and cheers grew like the rumbling of an earthquake. It grew louder and louder, inexorable like the tide at the nearby beach... No, like a tsunami!

Inebrio Shagaz stood on the steps of his presidential palace in the bright morning sunshine. The world press crowded around below, adjusting and clicking their cameras. Fortyish and stocky with slicked-down, black, Valentino-style hair, Inebrio stood at his full height of five foot one inch with his shoulders thrown back. He had learned long ago that if he stooped at all, he would look shorter. His black mustache crowned a wide mouth that opened like a trap, revealing rows of the perfectly capped, pearly white teeth of a modern politician. Today, he was the matador before his adoring public, receiving gratitude for the spectacle and the kill.

"I wish to hold this press conference in English as a tribute to the United States of America," he began. "Let me first announce that there was an attempted *coup d'état* last night by guerilla insurgents. They temporarily gained control of the electrical power and communications in Santo Domingo. Then they stormed the palace, attempting to kill me and my family, but they did not find us there. And because of their search and confusion, it gave time for the forces loyal to me to thwart the plot and arrest the leaders. My friends, what saved the Dominican Republic and my family as well was… Rachmaninoff. Yes, the composer, Sergei Rachmaninoff… and a program called Musical Emissaries sent to us by the U.S. government. You see, I wanted to hear a performance of my beloved Second Piano Concerto of Rachmaninoff at the amphitheater last night, so my security detail stole us away and put my family and me in one of the stalls. And what an evening it was. When the power was cut off, and there was no light, the brave American artist and musical emissary from the United States, Princess Little Feather Susquat, continued to play alone by flashlight as the audience and I sat transfixed. Had she not done that, I would have left and returned to the palace and my fate.

I would like to read a letter I have written to the president of the United States:

Dear Mr. President:

I wish to congratulate you, sir, on a new program in public diplomacy initiated under your administration. I refer to the Musical Emissary Program. Through that program, we in the Dominican Republic had the honor of hosting a gracious and brave artist who continued to give us joy and beauty in the midst of darkness and revolution. I give full credit to the Musical Emissary Program for keeping at bay those forces of panic, fear, and chaos that sought to destroy freedom in the Caribbean Basin."

CHAPTER SIX

*S*tuart Stadler, head of the press section, hurried through the courtyard and into the alcove that framed the entrance to Jason's suite of offices. He rang the buzzer while he looked at his reflection in the glass door. His goatee had not been trimmed that morning. It seemed as if he didn't have time to do anything. Another buzzer sounded, and he opened the door. The identification card around his neck swung on its chain while he plopped himself on a plush sofa in the receiving area of the office. His chest and belly rose and fell like a fast heartbeat. "Whew," he said, wiping his face.

Jason came out to meet him.

"I've never seen it like this. I mean, we're supposed to be an anchovy agency—very specialized. Some people don't like anchovies on their pizza. And then suddenly the whole damn country wants anchovies."

Marilyn crossed the room and seated herself on one of the soft leather chairs next to him.

Stuart felt like he was in somebody's private living room and made a mental note to come more often. "Nobody's supposed to know what we do, right? It's a secret." His eyes darted across the room. "I mean we're prohibited from telling the American people what we do because they might get propagandized if they bend over, so we do it overseas and call it—"

"What's going on?" Jason was frustrated. This guy was talking in riddles.

"You are hot, man! You've turned this agency on its ear."

Jason looked helplessly at Marilyn.

"Some coffee?" she asked.

"Coffee?" Stuart's shriek went like a dart to a board. "I've had a whole pot. I'm' so wired that—"

The phones rang. That was normal. But after they stopped, they rang again. That was not. The secretary came out of her office. She was a short, attractive, African American woman, subdued with well-coiffed hair and gold jewelry. She didn't wait until she reached the other three. "Mr. Angeletti, the White House is on one line, Director Cone's on the other, and NBC news is on a third."

Stuart nodded his head vigorously. "You see... You see! That's what I've been trying to—"

Jason walked calmly into his office, but Marilyn was frustrated. She would be on the outside of events for a few moments with nothing to do but wait with Stuart.

"I've never seen it like this." He shook his head, and his hair weave shimmied like a raccoon going up a tree.

Marilyn asked at a deliberately slow speed, "Stuart, what's going on?" She lisped slightly on the s's.

"The press! There are feature articles this morning on this Little Feather gal, on Jason, on the agency, on the Caribbean Basin, on guerillas, on... My office is going nuts trying to keep up with the inquiries. It's like a wildfire! This Santo Domingo thing really turns people on."

"Articles where, Stuart?"

"You name it: the *New York Times*, the *Chicago Tribune*, the *Los Angeles Times,* the *Wall Street Journal.* It's a firestorm!"

Jason came out of his office looking pale. He stood in front of the two of them for a moment, then sank into an arm chair. "The White House says the president wants me there when he receives the president of the Dominican Republic next week. And that he's going to give me an award."

Marilyn burst out in truncated, orgiastic chirps. "Oh! Jason...! WOW! Can I go, too?"

"Harry Cone just told me that the award should go to him since he's director of the agency, and that I should insist on that to the White House."

"You mean..." Marilyn paused. "That you're getting recognition from the president, but Mr. Cone isn't. Oh, Jason! I'm SO proud of you."

"I've been dealing with that." Stuart shook his mane of hair again. "Cone's been on the phone with me since early this morning. 'What the hell's going on?' he keeps asking."

"And finally," said Jason with resignation, "NBC news wants me to appear on *Meet the Washington Press*."

"Jason!" Marilyn shrieked. "That's the biggest Sunday morning political talk show."

"Harry Cone wanted to be on that one, too." Stuart rolled his eyes. "But the networks found out it was really Jason who created the program."

"It's all ridiculous." Jason bit his lip. "I don't want any of it. This is a high roller show for senators, congressmen, presidential candidates, current affairs... I'm not up to it. I'm an artist. I don't speak their jargon."

"That's not a problem." Stuart collected himself. "My office will brief you until you know your lines cold. We'll explore all possible questions and write out the answers. All you have to do is memorize them. But you have to look natural when you give it. We can help you with that, too."

Jason looked at Stuart's wire-rim glasses, small beady eyes, clothes that didn't match, and his hair. He thought Stuart Stadler looked as natural as an Astroturf lawn.

The next day, Marilyn brought in a copy of the *Washington Post*. "Another scandal, Jason. You're the only thing that's still running around here."

Jason opened the paper.

WASHINGTON, D.C.- Harold Cone, the controversial director of the International Cultural Communications Agency and the president's "closest friend" has been accused of making a list of 'undesirable Americans' who were to be permanently excluded from being sent overseas by the speaker program of the agency. This program enlists speakers to lecture abroad about, among other things, American foreign policy. The name of the program is "Carrying the Load of Democracy's Soldiers," and the participants were identified under the acronym, CLODS. Mr. Cone's alleged list of undesirables carries the names of some of Washington and the country's heaviest political hitters. Critics of Mr. Cone are comparing him to a dictator and accusing him of interfering with the free exchange of ideas. Others are asking, "When will he go?"

Jason drove to the event at the White House in his old Dodge with the dent in the side. It needed a paint job and had been parked mostly on the street. He managed to get Marilyn invited, but she wished they were arriving in a different vehicle.

"Why are we doing this?" she asked.

"Because I don't want to forget who I am."

"But you know who you are."

"It can slip away." He turned onto Pennsylvania Avenue. The name of the street used to thrill him, but it was all too familiar now. The luster had worn off.

"Are you trying to make some kind of statement?"

"What do you mean, Marilyn?"

"Some kind of populist, anti-government thing."

"I just didn't want to spend the money on a cab."

"Does this car really show respect to the president?" Marilyn folded her arms.

"He's not going to ride in it."

"You know what I mean."

"Look, how good can the president be, anyway, if Harry Cone is his best friend?"

"Jason!" Marilyn shrieked at the high decibel of a parakeet trying to get out of its cage. "Mr. Cone gave you this great job!"

"I know, I know, but he's not Paul Revere. I've had to fight all the way."

"Well what turns you on, anyway?"

"You do." He patted her knee. "And the concert at the Kennedy Center, and getting this program off the ground. Everything else in this town is a dog and pony show." He yawned.

Marilyn stared in disbelief. "You scare me, Jason."

"Why?"

"Sometimes I think you're dangerous."

"Dangerous to whom? To you? To Washington? To the country?"

"It's like you don't fit in."

"I don't."

They looked at each other for a moment.

At the White House gate, Jason gave both names and showed their drivers licenses. He was waved through and drove up the circular driveway. He stopped under the portico, and a marine guard with epaulets and white gloves opened his door. Another opened Marilyn's side.

"Welcome, Mr. Angeletti."

Marilyn looked at Jason, amazed. She mouthed the word "how."

"They had my license number," he whispered.

The two entered the White House Entrance Hall with its four great pillars and huge chandelier emblazoned with the Presidential Seal. Marilyn wore a tomato-red dress and simple string of pearls that complimented her natural beauty. Jason had on a pinstripe suit with a loud, yellow tie. They walked straight ahead on the shiny marble floor as if they knew where they were going, but were glad to follow everybody else into the Cross Hall toward the East Room.

Marilyn whispered, "Jason, there's Senator Pugwam, the chairman of the Foreign Relations Committee... and Senator Panzer." She trembled as they walked into the East Room with its high windows and gold drapes. The custom-made Steinway piano was there, with brocade on its side and the strong-chested, sculpted eagles serving as legs at either end. She cupped her hand over his ear. "Did you know this is where President Lincoln lay in state?"

"Yes, I knew that." He smiled.

"Jason, this is the greatest day of my life."

There were rows of comfortable, straight-back chairs lined up. The chief usher showed Marilyn and Jason to seats in the front row, directly opposite the podium.

Marilyn nudged Jason. "There's Mr. Cone, over by the entrance."

Jason turned.

Harry stood immaculately groomed in a thousand-dollar suit from Savile Row and presidential cuff links. He was looking around as though wanting to be in the center of everything.

The chief of staff came over, fixing his gaze on Harry like a prosecutor at a trial. "It's getting a little old, Harry, all these scandals. And now another one! It's starting to embarrass the president. I thought you'd have cleaned up your act by now."

Harry tried to move his face into the other man's but had to look up. "You go ahead and talk to the president about me, and maybe you already have. But then I'll talk to him about you. The difference is that you're a hireling, and I'm his best friend. You talk to him during business hours, and I can talk to him anytime, like maybe over Thanksgiving dinner for the whole damn day. We'll see which one of us goes first." Harry backed away from the space he had usurped. "And besides, he likes my jokes. You probably haven't got any that are worth a damn." He turned and ducked through a door that led to the green room.

The glare from the television lights signaled something was

about to begin. News reporters with cameras walked around the periphery of the podium. The president came out from the green room. Marilyn's body stiffened as though at attention. There was applause as the tall, elderly man, with an American flag on the lapel of his perfectly pressed suit, walked to the podium. Behind him were Inebrio Shagaz, the president of the Dominican Republic, and Harry Cone. The two stood smiling, Harry, because he was about four inches taller than Inebrio, and the other because he liked where his life had brought him. They both had wide smiles with rows of ivory that could have made a two-piano team. The president seemed cheerful. There was a genial quality to the way he read from the cue cards.

"Ladies and gentlemen, my fellow Americans. I'm proud to have as my guest today a man who has stood up for the values that we Americans believe in. President Inebrio Shagaz has shown the world that we don't have to accept insurgent guerillas who threaten our future and stability. With great courage to lead, he has allowed the Caribbean Basin to survive in freedom, and this has sent a message of hope to all of Latin America."

There was applause as Inebrio moved behind the podium, but suddenly his body disappeared. All that could be seen was his head. "Mr. President, I have said publicly and have told you as well that I owe all the success of defeating the insurgency in the Caribbean to the United States of America and its wonderful Musical Emissary Program. That story has been told over and over in the media, so I won't repeat it here, but I wish to salute you and your good judgment in offering to the world the best side of America. And I salute also Mr. Harry Cone, who is the director of the ICCA which handles public diplomacy for the United States."

More applause echoed through the room.

The president moved back to the podium. "Let's hear something now from Mr. Cone. This is a man who has been stellar in bringing the best of America to the world—a great American, a great leader in public diplomacy, and a great human being."

Harry moved up to the mic and gleefully raised it to his height. "Thank you, Mr. President. It's a privilege to be here. At my age, it's a privilege to be anywhere."

The president chuckled. Only a few in the audience did.

"I also want to thank the president for saying those kind things about me. All of them, of course, are true." He crinkled his face into a grin. "It reminds me of the man who said he was perfect and never made a mistake. He thought he did once, but he was wrong."

The president roared, but the audience sat impassively.

"As many of you know, the president and I are old friends. And we've finally reached an age when our secrets are safe with our friends because they can't remember them."

The president, still laughing, slapped Harry on the back and moved back to the mic. "You see now why we need Harry around here?"

Only one or two people nodded.

"Now we come to the reason we're all here. We want to recognize the young man who created this wonderful Musical Emissary Program. You've heard President Shagaz talk about it earlier, and no doubt you've read about it. Now, you can see for yourselves the man responsible for it, the hero of the hour, Mr. Jason Angeletti."

More applause came from the audience.

Jason walked up, and the president extended his hand.

"Jason, I want to present you with a presidential award given only to those who have furthered the cause of freedom over-seas on behalf of the United States."

Applause.

Jason took the award and almost dropped it, a heavily framed certificate with all kinds of signatures. He looked at it and saw his name was misspelled.

"I truly believe," the president continued, "that small things can indicate judgment. And I couldn't help noticing a beautiful woman sitting next to you here in the first row! If that's an example of your judgment, then no wonder we're honoring you here today."

Applause was louder this time.

Marilyn gripped her chair tightly.

Jason moved to the microphone. "Thank you, Mr. President. I'm sure Marilyn is more than pleased with your comment. But it reminds me of the story of the man who stood up at his own testimonial and said that he'd been in love with the same woman for twenty-five years, and if his wife found out she'd kill him."

The president had a stunned look. He stared for a moment, raised his eyebrows, and let out a belly laugh. The audience followed suit.

Harry Cone looked puzzled and slightly menaced. Jokes were his territory. The president kept laughing. Harry moved in front of Inebrio and across to the podium, blurting into the mic, "And he takes her everywhere, but she keeps finding her way back."

The president couldn't stop laughing.

Jason stood in front of the mic. "She asked me to take her somewhere she'd never been, so I said, 'Try the kitchen.'"

Now the president doubled up, laughing in short gasps. A member of the secret service moved in quickly, pushing Jason aside and grabbed the president, trying to determine if he was sick or had been injured. Tears were rolling down the chief executive's face. He tried to get his breath.

Harry stepped on Inebrio's foot as he groped toward the

microphone again. "My bride was only fifteen when we married, but that's a hundred and five in dog years."

Jason calmly moved in front of Harry. "I fell in love with a psychic, but she ended it before we met."

The president went down on all fours and beat the floor with the palm of his hand. His laughter came in short spurts of sobbing, high-pitch gasps. Photographers rushed like an invading army to flash pictures.

Harry looked at Jason with contempt, as though he had found the secret password. "Don't fart higher than your ass," he said. Then he leaned over the president's supine body on the floor. "Two flies were flying around, and one fly said to the other, 'Hey, fly! Your man's open.'"

The president's breath was spent. He lay on the floor, looking up at the ceiling. "Harry," he said, barely audible. "You've already told me that one."

Marilyn came into Jason's office the next morning, looking haggard for the first time in her life. Sad and disillusioned, she threw a stack of newspapers on his desk.

"There it is," she said. "It's all there!"

Jason didn't even need to open the papers. Everything was on the front page. He looked at the photo in the *New*

York Times. The president was down on his hands and knees in the East Room. The caption read: *What's wrong with this picture.* the *Wall Street Journal* featured the same photo with the caption: *Is this man fit to lead?* But the worst was the *New York Daily News* which had the president down on all fours with a simple, one-word caption: *Woof!*

"Why did you do this?" Marilyn stood behind his chair with the cold fury of an assassin.

He turned halfway around to see if her face matched the voice. "Do what?"

"Destroy his presidency."

"What!"

"That's what the *Los Angeles Times* says. *'Who would vote for a president that crawls around the East Room of the White House on all fours?'* Here, read it!"

"Why are you putting all this on me?"

"Where did you get those jokes from, Jason?"

"From Harry Cone. That's all he ever did during those piano lessons I gave him years ago—tell jokes. He never practiced and couldn't really play, so he'd tell jokes."

"And why did you decide to use this particular occasion to go through your repertoire?"

"Because I thought it would help in relating to the president. I can't do that other blah-blah jargon."

"But this is the president of the United States. He could be finished because of this, along with all his wonderful ideas. And then we're finished, too. If he goes, we go. Don't you realize that?"

"Marilyn, you make it seem like I plotted this whole thing. How could I have known the guy is a laughaholic?"

"I just don't think you respect the whole thing. How many people get to be honored at the White House anyway?"

"Look, Marilyn, maybe I am crazy, but if so, I wasn't the only one up there that is. How do you deal with that?"

"With respect! These people have power, and there's a reason they do."

"Marilyn, maybe some of your heroes have clay feet."

"And maybe I'm looking at one right now." She walked out with her spiked heels grinding into the carpet and slammed the door to her office.

Jason sat, pensive and empty. Was this the end? He got up and went into the lounge area to his favorite chair. He wormed his backside into the plush leather and put his feet up on the table. What now? Would she leave? Would he have to fire her?

The secretary was out for the day, so the program coordinator answered the phone—a tall, Asian American woman whose deference blended into the beige walls. She approached him from across the room. "Mr. Angeletti, it's an important call." But her voice was singsong and high pitched, like a little girl's with no resonance.

He could never quite hear her so, out of politeness, always moved closer before asking her to repeat what she had just said. This time, he had to travel across the room. *Pain in the ass*, he thought. *Maybe I ought to get rid of her too.*

"It's Mr. Barron."

"Could you repeat that?"

"Mr. Barron's office just called! He's on his way down here with Mr. Stadler. They want to meet with you."

The buzzer sounded, and two men walked purposefully through the security door. Stuart Stadler was moving more resolutely than usual, the by-product of a civil service employee being in such close physical proximity to power.

Besides Harry Cone, the man in front of him was the most feared in the agency. Bill Barron had survived on the high wire by being Harry's closest adviser and enforcer. The scar across the side of his face was not from bureaucratic infighting but rather a childhood accident. But it served him well. His mouth took on a crooked smile. "I have to say that you and Miss Goodrump have done quite a job with this little program. Everybody thinks it's great, and it makes the agency look good." His steel-grey eyes looked around the room like a saloon keeper surveying the evening house. Then they focused on Jason. "That's why you're still here, even though you tell funny jokes to the president. Otherwise, you'd be gone in a New York minute."

Stuart Stadler's eyes started blinking uncontrollably.

Barron walked over to the secretary's desk and casually opened a folder, then closed it. He looked up at the nameplate on Marilyn's door. "A real mom-and-pop operation, huh? Not too many of those in the government. That can make for efficiency. But of course it depends on how everybody gets along. You guys are professionals, though, so you make it happen. That's good. Maybe we should put you in for a model employees award." He eyed Jason sideways to determine what impact his remarks were making.

Marilyn liked awards; Jason thought it might be an opening to bring her out. "Speaking of 'mom and pop,'" he said lamely, "let's bring 'Mom' out." They walked over to her door, and he knocked gently. "Marilyn? Bill Barron is here with Stuart Stadler. Would you like to say hello?"

"GET LOST!"

Even though there was no echo or any kind of reverberation, the muffled words hung in the stuffy air. Jason looked at the two men and shrugged his shoulders. "Burn out, I guess."

Barron nodded toward the chairs in the lounge. "We need to talk about Sunday, Jason."

"What's Sunday?" Jason was planning a day in bed with the newspaper.

Barron looked astonished. *"Meet the Washington Press!* You're on TV doing a ten-minute piece on public diplomacy. Aren't too many people that would forget about that."

"The biggest news show on television!" said Stuart Stadler, nodding his head. It was safe to make a declarative sentence about a fact that would not likely be disputed. He felt comfortable in being strong about it.

"But you've got to know what to say." Barron put on a poker face. His scar was immobile. "We're here to brief you."

As if on cue, Stuart opened his briefcase and took out a sheaf of paper. "These are a list of questions we anticipate from the press, and underneath, we've written the answers that we'd like you to give. You'll have to commit them to memory though."

Bill moved to the edge of his seat and pointed his finger. "And it's got to look natural!"

"Natural!" Stuart Stadler nodded again. He handed Jason the piece of paper.

Marilyn opened her door and glided softly through the lounge area, sinking unobtrusively into a chair. No one took notice.

Bill Barron continued. "We hope you will see fit to honor the director in some way in front of millions of Americans. He continues to believe, as do many of us, that he should have been asked to appear as well. But you'll have to carry the banner."

Jason looked at the first question and answer on the paper.

(Q) Have you felt personally touched by any of the recent controversies surrounding Director Harry Cone?

(A) Director Cone has been so extraordinary in his capacity as a leader that it has been a privilege to work with him. His brilliance yet common-sense insight into the world and its problems make every day spent with him a peculiar gift. Controversies have no relevance where Director Cone is concerned.

Jason felt disgusted. This was hogwash! He looked at the next one.

(Q) Do you or Director Cone feel in any way responsible for the president's declining poll numbers after the White House incident where he apparently couldn't stop laughing?

(A) Director Cone's very special relationship with the president is out of bounds to the public. But I can tell you that they have both worked closely together for the good of the country. Mr. Cone's sage advice is much

sought after, and he has contributed to all good things
that have happened to our country under this presi-
dent. We couldn't do better than having Harry Cone
working closely with the president for our welfare.
Sleep safely, America! (Here, look at the camera
and smile.)

Jason counted seven more sheets of paper with a sum of twenty-five questions and answers.

"How long do you think it'll take you to memorize all this?" Barron's voice broke through like the blare of rush hour traffic sounds.

"I... I don't know."

"I'll help him with it." Marilyn's face was set. "This is one more big opportunity that's come Jason's way, and he'd better get it right."

"I can help too." Stuart looked eager. "We'll go for breakfast at the Hawk 'n' Dove on Sunday morning, do a dress rehearsal, and I'll have their studio limousine pick us up from there and drive us to the set."

Marilyn no longer slept with him on the weekends, so it was easier to get going, get in the bathroom, and get ready. He looked at himself in the mirror. He asked the reflection how he

could get up in front of a camera and lie—probably wouldn't
be able to. But it wasn't a voice that answered; it was his gut.
He went into the closet to pick out a bright tie. He had heard
strong colors worked better on television. He tied the knot and
faced himself again in the mirror. There was still shaving
cream on his face. He pleaded to the mirror that he had tried to
memorize the answers, but they were absurd.

It was a four-block walk to the restaurant. He walked along in
an agitated state. It was not the same anxiety as before a
performance but more from the awareness of possibly losing a
friend—himself. How could he live with his person if he
didn't respect it? His pace rounded historic federal-style town-
houses that were being restored, row houses, and some brown-
stones. Sunday morning was casual on Capitol Hill. People
walked their dogs in sweat suits, and kids played in the small
park. He came to Pennsylvania Avenue. Cars were double
parked, and people were going into cafés and bookstores. He
turned right at the intersection and walked into the Hawk 'n'
Dove. Every table seemed taken. Then he noticed Marilyn and
Stuart seated in the back.

"You look pale." Stuart extended his meaty hand warily. "Are
you all right?" He had to get Jason through this in an acceptable way.

"I'm a little shaky."

"How about a mimosa?"

"What's that?"

"Champagne and orange juice," Marilyn answered. She was glad she finally knew something he didn't.

"No thanks."

"Jason, I brought another question and answer that wasn't in your briefing papers. You'd better study it. We think it goes well."

Stuart pulled a crinkly piece of paper out of his vest pocket and passed it to Jason over the water glass.

(Q) How important has Harry Cone been to public diplomacy in the long term?

(A) As the sun energizes the earth beneath it, so too the head of a large corporation or federal agency provides the light for those to see and work around him. As in one body, when the feet are struck, the head feels the pain and vice versa. The farther one gets from Mr. Cone, who is the sun, the colder the extremities become, but the closer we all get to him, the more we feel part of the same solar system.

Jason looked up. "Who wrote this?"

"I did this very morning. And the director personally approved it." He tried to stick out his chest, but his belly hit the table first.

"I think I will take that mimosa." Jason felt trapped.

"I'll get it." Stuart pushed his chair back.

Jason looked at Marilyn. "I guess I don't have to ask where you are in all of this?"

Her face was granite. "Have any of the recent controversies surrounding Director Cone touched you personally?"

"That's from the Q & A list."

"This is a rehearsal. What's the answer?"

"Oh, hell!"

"You haven't even studied them, have you!"

Stuart came back with Jason's drink, and they ordered scrambled eggs.

The mimosa went down pretty smoothly, with citrus and bubbles. Stuart and Marilyn talked about how important the broadcast was.

"Say, Jason, you still look a little pale. Did that drink help?"

"Not much, Stuart."

"We can try another one."

Marilyn furled her eyebrows. She watched Stuart go back to the bar. "Be careful."

The second drink came with a hot cross bun.

"You know, Jason, if you do everything right today, you'll be a hero." Stuart pushed the drink toward him.

"Really?"

"And this might be your last chance." Marilyn's icy edge was intended to have double meaning.

He finished the mimosa and suggested they leave. "Show time," he said.

Stuart came back with a cup in his hand. "For the road."

Jason stumbled getting into the limousine but managed to slide across the length of the back seat behind the driver. Marilyn sat as far at the other end as she could.

When the car drove away, Stuart handed him the cup. "More orange juice," he said.

Jason played with it, rolling it around in his hand as they crossed K Street. Then he took out a toothpick and picked at his teeth. When they turned left on M Street, he absentmindedly took a sip. And then another. By the time they arrived at the studios, he was asleep. The doors opening on the passenger side woke him up. He tried to open his own door but had trouble. One of the network staff opened it, but he couldn't get out. When they finally stood him up against the car, he was afraid to let go. They brought a wheelchair to bring him into the greenroom since there was a long corridor.

Marilyn looked at Stuart. "He's drunk. What did you put in those drinks?"

"They were double vodkas; that's all."

"What!" she screamed. "Why?"

"The guy's uptight. I know what that's like. I can't go into an executive committee meeting with Harry Cone unless I've had some doubles."

The greenroom room was hot, so Jason asked for water. Everything was spinning. A buzzer went off, and someone said, "We'll have to take him like that."

They wheeled him down a narrow causeway into the studio, a cavernous dark room where TV lights lit up one of the rear corners. He was helped to a table where four men sat wearing makeup. They looked at him. A red light went on and the cameramen began a countdown, forcefully gesturing toward the men. It seemed like Judgment Day—everything in an instant.

Jason looked at the control room where Marilyn and Stuart were sitting. It came through in a hazel blush and seemed so far away. He turned toward the moderator who appeared to be wearing a halo.

"Good morning, ladies and gentlemen, and welcome to *Meet the Washington Press.* This morning we have the creator of the Musical Emissary Program, the classical music exchange program sponsored by our government that you may have read about. It's been credited by the president of the Dominican Republic as having saved freedom and democracy in the Caribbean Basin. So we welcome to the show this morning, Mr. Jason Angeletti."

A large camera moved toward Jason. He looked at it suspiciously, gripping the end of the table with both hands to keep from swaying. All ten fingers held on so tightly that the circulation stopped.

"Mr. Angeletti, our first question will come from Ardell Longine of the *Wall Street Journal.*"

Ardell coughed with a smoker's rattle.

"Mr. Angeletti, have any of Mr. Cone's recent scandals touched you personally in any way?"

I… I wouldn't let him touch me." Jason licked his lips and felt thirsty.

All four journalists looked at each other. Ardell tried to keep it moving. "Mr. Angeletti, do you anticipate doing any more public diplomacy initiatives in the arts since you have been so successful with this one."

The upper part of Jason's torso moved back in the chair, but it made him nauseous, so he pulled himself back to the table. "Well, two are better than one, but one is good, too."

Marilyn Goodrump sat in the control booth with her hands over her face.

The camera moved to the second journalist.

"Mr. Angeletti, do you feel personally responsible for the president's low poll numbers due to that embarrassing laugh fest at the White House."

Jason burped slightly. "I was funnier than he was."

The pace quickened.

"Mr. Angeletti, we know you've been acquainted with Mr. Cone for many years, but were you also acquainted with the president previously?"

"Yes and no." He tried to stay upright.

"Could you explain, sir?"

"Well, I never met him, but I know him because all the robots in this town wear the same suits."

The control room looked like a wax museum as people locked into fixed positions. Stuart Stadler's jaw dropped. His body went rigid, and his eyes looked straight ahead as though staring into an abyss. Marilyn buried her head in her arms.

Ardell Longine asked another question. "Mr. Angeletti, your boss, Harold Cone, has come under a lot of criticism in this town. I wonder if you could tell us your opinion. Putting your personal relationship aside, do you think Mr. Cone has done a good job as director of the International Cultural Communications Agency?"

Jason's teeth itched. He wanted his toothpick. "Uh... Mr. Cone has done as good a job as he is capable of doing. That's why you should all lock your doors at night." He got out his toothpick.

"I'm Morton Pepto of the *Los Angeles Times*. There is a rumor that Princess Little Feather Susquat, the recent musical emissary, may be tapped to be ambassador to the Dominican Republic. Is there any smoke there?"

"That would be like Mother Goose going to Cuba." Jason started to perspire.

"Are you stating that there will be a new ambassador to Cuba and that we will normalize relations? Who is Mother Goose?"

"You must have been a deprived child."

The moderator, sensing some news, decided to close the show. "Mr. Angeletti, would you like to say something to the millions of Americans who are watching out there?"

Jason turned toward one of the cameras. "Folks, you're not going to get anything out of this. People come to this town to make a name for themselves, not to do anything for you."

They wheeled him into the control room where Stuart Stadler sat, frozen and transfixed.

Jason broke the mood. "Where's Marilyn?"

Stuart turned slowly, like some piece of heavy machinery. "She left you a message. One word only: GONE."

"Take me back home, then."

The ride in the limousine was quiet. They both sat in the back seat, Stuart watching his whole life pass before him. "They're going to blame me for this," he kept repeating. "I'm finished. There's nothing more."

Jason thought this was the time in the movie when the grieved person is handed a revolver to do the honorable thing.

The next morning dawned like any other. Jason was still alive and so, presumably, was everybody else. He went into work because he had nothing else to do. Would he be strung up, crucified? Would his desk still be there?

The secretary was the only one in. Marilyn and the program coordinator had already sought transfers to other offices, according to the personnel papers on his desk. The finality of it made him sad; it would never be the same. There was also a message from Stuart Stadler, saying he was coming down for a meeting. Jason wondered if Stuart ever thought to ask if he was free for a meeting, or if Jason even wanted to see him. He didn't, so maybe he'd go for a walk. But it was too late.

Coming through the security door with an armful of newspapers, Stuart's head led the rest of his squat body like a reptile trying to reach out of its shell. His identification card swung violently on its chain. He plopped the papers on Jason's desk.

"You did it again. Boy, are you a sleeper! How in the hell do you manage to break all the rules and come out smelling like a rose!"

Stuart had highlighted various columns and editorials so Jason could read them.

Los Angeles Times
"Finally Truth to Power With Jason Angeletti."

The Wall Street Journal
"Angeletti Speaks Simple Words of Fact. America's Sick of Washington!"

The New York Times
"Protect This Whistle-blower. We Need Purity and Comity in Washington."

The Chicago Tribune
"Jason Angeletti says the 'emperor has no clothes.' What's wrong with that statement? Answer: Nobody else in Washington had the courage to say it. The heartland of America is with Jason Angeletti."

The New York Post
"Godzilla With Angel Wings."

Stuart looked at Jason with a smirk. "Harry Cone wanted to

fire you last night, and the paperwork was even done, but it didn't go forward this morning because you're a sensation—not in Washington, but out there in the country with the great unwashed. There's too much support nationwide." He glanced at Marilyn's office. "But you'll have to get a new team. Her paperwork did go through."

He didn't want to admit that he missed Marilyn, but in his mind's eye, he saw her everywhere. He felt alone and depressed but had to keep going, although he didn't know why. He supposed there was nothing else to do. He hung his head for a while, until he noticed phone messages on his desk. He thumbed through them idly. One was from Edmund O'Rourke, and it came from the White House.

"Ed, what are you doing over there?"

"A new job. I'm in White House Communications."

"Congratulations!"

"Listen, Jason, I've been tasked to give you some bad tidings. Your political brethren aren't happy. They blame that White House incident last week and the president's falling support on you."

"What did I have to do with it?"

"You told the jokes that got him in trouble. His poll numbers are falling so rapidly that he might not recover from this politically. And if he loses the upcoming election, we all lose our jobs."

"But I can't help it if the president's addicted to one-liners."

"Jason, I'm just worried that nobody's going to be willing to go out on a limb for you anymore."

Within days, Jason began feeling the isolation. Word had gone out, and already the old support group was dwindling. Many of whom he had relied on were now unresponsive. Even the political appointees closed ranks and were talking only behind closed doors.

The phone rang. "Mr. Angeletti, Clark Kreig would like to see you this afternoon if it's convenient." Jason's secretary was always appropriate.

"Tell him I'll be right up."

Clark was technically his supervisor, but he rarely heard from him. Jason was not really supervised by anyone since no one there knew enough about music. *What is this about, then?* As he walked into the office, he thought about Clark's facial tics and wondered if he would have to get used to them all over again. They began almost immediately.

"My God, you're hot property!" Clark's head made a full circle and then went back to its starting point. "You're the only guy Harry Cone and the party would like to get rid of but can't. You've got too much support across the country, and, on top of that, the program you started has been a success." Clark shook his head as he pondered the enormity of it. But the shaking started to accelerate until his head seemed to vibrate. Then, with a jolt, it came to a stop. "You really ought to leave."

"What?"

"The country, I mean. We'll send you on an official trip over-seas until things cool down. Outta sight, outta mind." Clark turned toward his shoulder, his teeth chattering while his head jerked up and down, before returning to normal position. Jason had seen that one before and called it the 'bite the parrot.'

He took a deep breath. He was exhausted. "I'd like to play while I'm over there."

"Makes sense. You're the director of the program, so that'll show everyone that you can do what you send other people out to do. Where do you want to go?"

"I don't know. Maybe South America? But I'll need to practice."

"Why? Don't you know any pieces? We need to do this quickly."

"I have to get my fingers, ear, brain, and heart all working together."

"Sounds like an autopsy. How long do you need?"

"Depends on how much time I have to practice. I'm in the office all day, you know."

"You live nearby, so take a longer lunch break and practice the piano at home. But do a memo to me and catalogue all the hours you put in. Then, if any questions come up, I can make the case that it's in preparation for an official trip. Don't take longer than two months. I can't stretch it out beyond then... and keep your head down in the meantime. No auditions or anything. Not a peep!"

"I couldn't do anything if I wanted. I no longer have a staff."

"When you get back, you may no longer have a job. Let's hope this works."

It was one month later and the day before his trip when he came in with the memo. Clark looked at it. His head went down to his chest and then back up like it was on a trampoline. "My God! Three hundred seventy-five hours. I don't think I've put that much time in raising my kid. I thought you musicians just woke up in the morning and played something. I guess not, huh? Tell me, how long are these recitals anyway?"

"Eighty or ninety minutes of music," replied Jason.

"That's not all memorized, is it?"

"Yes."

"Well, how do you do that? Write it on your sleeve?"

CHAPTER SEVEN

$\mathcal{T}$he plane lowered gently over the coastline of Rio de Janeiro. Jason had always wanted to visit there, to see Christ on the mountain and the beach at Ipanema. Once, he had seen an old movie that was filmed in Rio. The city looked good even in black and white. Now, it was breathtaking with mountains rising out of the water and palm trees dotting endless beachlines. He imagined himself dancing across the ballroom of the Hotel Copacabana, like in that movie. Perhaps he could find a Brazilian beauty to do the bossa nova. The lights were flickering in the *favela* behind the skyline of the city as dusk settled over the mountains. *This could be the start of something new*, he thought. And then there was Walter Kinderscenen, the branch cultural affairs officer. An unusual Foreign Service Officer, Wally was fun to be around. He cared little for the Foreign Service taboo of not going native. Wally blended in wherever he was assigned. It would be a relief after Washington. Yes, Jason had chosen well to come to Rio.

In the lounge area of the airport, there was a young woman holding a sign with Jason's name on it. She had braces, and the man next to her, an earring.

"Hello there! We're here for Walter." She raised her arm in a cheer, and the man gave a thumbs-up.

The driver took Jason's bags and put them in the car while the other two held hands. The car sped off.

"Welcome to Rio," she said.

"Who are you?"

"I'm a junior Foreign Service Officer. Kind of an intern down here working with Walter, and it's great.

Jason looked at her companion.

"Oh, that's my boyfriend. He's been down from the states for a month now, and he goes everywhere with me."

Jason had to get used to the situation. These two seemed incongruent with the outward seriousness of the black government limousine, and the briefing papers on her lap didn't look like they belonged there. She and her boyfriend looked more like recreation directors at a singles resort. Walter must be running an even looser operation than he imagined. He looked at the driver and saw the biggest neck he had ever witnessed—

bulging muscles in a tight-fitting suit and the jet-black hair of an Indian.

"That's Yucca, your bodyguard," said the girl.

"Bodyguard?"

"Yeah, Rio's a super dangerous place. You'll need Yucca."

Jason looked at the beautiful scenery as they sped down the freeway between the beaches and the sprawling city.

"Don't let that fool you." She gave him a knowing glance. "It's beautiful and seductive but very unsafe."

Her boyfriend nodded. His earring glistened as the sun darted out from a cloud and pierced the backseat window.

"Now, we have to brief you."

"What do you mean, 'we'?"

"Well, I have to," she said, correcting herself. Her boyfriend nodded again.

"Walter wanted me to do it before we arrive at his place. And he's been so good to Leroy and me that I want to do everything right. Okay, are you ready?"

"Ready."

"First off, make sure that you always carry identification on your person at all times."

"You mean my passport?"

"Not necessarily. Someone could steal that and sell it on the black market. I mean just anything that has your name and address on it, like a business card."

"Why?"

"In case they find your body."

The driver picked up speed. Jason felt like he was in a fortress.

"Don't wear anything shiny, like a wristwatch or rings. That sets them off; it's like a signal. They get excited."

Jason thought she was remarkably cheerful, considering the subject matter. "Well, at least we can enjoy the beaches," he said.

"Just don't walk on them."

"Why?"

"There's a larva that attaches itself to your skin. It's in the sand, and it's real hard to get rid of it."

Her boyfriend leaned over. "That's if you can get through all the dog shit."

She smiled at Leroy in appreciation. "And don't put your hand in the water," she said. "There's generations of sewage dumped right off the coast."

Jason felt clammy. "Where's my hotel?"

"You'll be in a good hotel, but don't go outside of it alone.

There are marauding gangs just waiting for tourists. Walter says to go no farther than the lobby."

"I think I need a drink."

"You can have a drink, but don't use ice. The water is full of bacteria. And raw vegetables are out; they use human fertilizer down here."

The car pulled into the driveway of a large home, almost an estate.

"We're here. Walter's waiting for you."

Jason didn't feel like getting out of the car, but he got out anyway. A servant met them in the doorway and showed them into the dining room.

Walter Kinderscenen was toasting a table of local guests with some dark red wine. One of the guests toasted Walter in return, then they toasted each other. This went on for a few minutes until the bottle was empty.

The girl interrupted. "Walter, Jason Angeletti is here."

Walter wheeled around. "Jason, how are you, fella! How about a drink? This is a thirty-three-year-old Portuguese port, nothing but the best. I'll have 'em bring another bottle."

"Walter, I've got to get to a piano. I've got a concert in three days, remember?"

"A piano? Don't you know your pieces yet?"

"It's like an athlete, Walter. We have to train every day."

"I'll be damned. I'd better find one!"

Walter did find one—in a museum. And Yucca sat through the rehearsals each day, never leaving Jason out of his sight. He sat impassively like a huge boulder, his chiseled face revealing nothing.

Rio was already getting routine. Each day was the same: back and forth from the hotel to practice. Yucca would meet him in the hotel lobby and take him down the steps to the car. They would traverse the city to the museum, and Yucca would take him from the parking lot to the elevator. The piano was on the top floor. Then, they'd go back to the hotel for Jason to have dinner that evening, alone. He felt like someone in the Federal Witness Protection Program. To break the routine, he asked Yucca if he could walk along one of the beaches—on the sidewalk of course. Yucca allowed it for about one hundred yards. Jason looked forward to the concert like a prison break.

It was held at the Sala Cecília Meireles, a prestigious recital hall in Rio de Janeiro. It had been acoustically refurbished and boasted one of the best concert grand pianos in all of South America. Jason hadn't had much time to prepare, but still it was like a dream to play on an international stage.

He settled into the opening of the concert quickly. He wasn't that nervous. He didn't know anyone in the audience, and that seemed to help. It was a catharsis, too, to be somewhere besides his hotel room. He warmed to the instrument. The sound was lively, easily heard, and he did not have to push it. After intermission, he was so relaxed that it felt like being in his own living room. Everything seemed easy. He improvised around the structure of the music, spontaneous and inspired.

It was in the closing group of Russian pieces, which he had specially chosen, that he went beyond himself. He entered their character, and the passion spent belied his modest and earnest stage presence. In an Étude-Tableau of Rachmaninoff, the melody sobbed, not like the waling of a professional mourner but with a steady drumbeat of sadness—respectable, well-modulated tears that people try to avoid in public but are somehow manageable. The bass and deep octaves of the Steinway created an organ roundness that grumbled and vibrated in the hall. Harmonies unveiled, snaked up the walls of the Sala Cecília Mereiles, winding around the great ceiling, and settling on the audience below. From the treble of the piano, every timber of the orchestra and of life could be heard: oboes, flutes, violins, sleigh bells, and the cold desolation of a Russian winter.

People were enthralled. In one of the lead papers of Rio de Janeiro, *Jornal do Brasil,* a critic wrote: "Jason Angeletti played Russian music like a true Russian."

The next day in an interview, he was asked to what he attributed his affinity for Russian music. "A performing artist must be an actor, a chameleon," he answered. "With Debussy, I am French; with Chopin, a Pole; Beethoven, a German; and when I play Rachmaninoff, I am completely Russian."

That seemed to suffice.

Walter Kinderscenen was so impressed, he planned a big party in Jason's honor. It would be one of his guest's few outings in Rio. Jason noticed more about Walter's house this time. It was at the base of Sugarloaf Mountain, in a prime area. He had a large household staff, as did most cultural affairs officers overseas, and he put them to good use, entertaining key contacts. Walter was the highest-ranking ICCA officer in Rio. Since it was only a branch post, he had no competition from the embassy, which was far away in Brasília.

The party started at noon. Jason arrived early, but there were already people there, and a guitarist was playing in the background. He walked through the house past the kitchen, where two heavyset women were cooking over a cauldron. They perspired heavily from the heat while stirring with wooden paddles. It was not appetizing. Walter gave him a drink.

"What are they fixing?" Jason asked.

"*Feijoada*," said Walter.

"What's that?"

"The national dish."

"What's in it?"

"Everything you're not supposed to have. Be sure and suck on an orange or lemon with it. That'll cut the grease. But I'll say one thing, you're going to get the real thing here. We're not skimping, and we're certainly not listening to those health nuts back in the states."

Jason tried his drink. It was pleasant but unlike anything he'd had before. "What's this called?" He held it up.

"That's a *caipirinha*. It's made with Brazilian rum called cachaça mixed with lime and granulated sugar. Be careful, it's strong!"

Jason took another sip. A porter in a white coat with a pitcher came up behind him. He filled Jason's glass back up to the top and did the same with each guest. As soon as anyone had a sip or two, he would reappear with the pitcher. No one ever had a glass that was less than full.

"How long is this party going to last, Walter?"

"Till people can't stand up anymore."

It was about the middle of the afternoon when they finally served the food. Jason had struck up a conversation with a government grantee who was the director of a theater institute in Vermont.

"What is this dish called *feijoada* anyway?" Jason asked.

The man tried to concentrate on the question but was distracted by the effects of all the rum he had consumed. "As far as I can figure out, it's got fat from every animal that ever walked the earth. I watched those hot, sweaty women cook that thing until I couldn't stand it any longer. You wouldn't believe what they put in there."

"Try me."

"Well, it's basically got about eight things in it." The man held up ten fingers. "First, you've got your black beans, then you've got your tongue."

"What?"

"Well, not your tongue but somebody's tongue, or some animal or something. Then you've got your lard, and your salted dried meat, and salt pork, and pork meat, and your pork ribs and sausages, and I'm telling you, it's enough to make you puke. And do you know what they serve with it? A green, leafy vegetable, as though that's supposed to make it all right. And then, so you don't have a coronary, you're supposed to suck on an orange between bites. Great, right?"

The man drank his *caipirinha* down fast, emptying the glass before the porter could get to it.

"A little contest I have with this guy," he said.

The porter steadied the man's hand so he could fill it back to the top.

"What do you think of these drinks?" Jason asked.

"Sweet but lethal. But mostly sweet." The man looked at his glass. "If you get sick on these, you'll throw up a candy cane."

Early the next morning, the day of Jason's departure from

Brazil, the phone rang in his room. He awoke with a bloated feeling, like he had swallowed a bowling ball. His head felt even worse, like it was caught between two anvils. This may have been the worst hangover of his life. The phone kept ringing. To make sure he was still alive, he dragged himself over to the window and looked at the ocean. It was still dark outside, but he could see the rolling motion of the waves, which reminded him of his stomach.

He finally picked up the phone. It was the embassy. There would be a national airline strike beginning later that morning, and planes would be grounded for days. He had to leave immediately to get the last plane out of Rio. A cable had already been sent to his next stop, Montevideo, Uruguay, notifying the embassy of his early arrival.

The flight to Montevideo was only a couple hours, but it might as well have been days. If time were suspended, it could have been purgatory. The sound of the engines and the dipping of the small plane in and out of air pockets felt like never-ending torture. When it finally landed, Jason moved like a broken-down procession toward the baggage claim area. He felt like an old man. Since there was no one to meet him at the airport, he had to take a cab into Montevideo.

"I was there. I really was! I just can't figure out how we missed each other." The cultural affairs officer was pale and slight, with a nose that narrowed to a sharp point at its end. He shepherded Jason around on his courtesy calls the next day.

The most important stop was to visit the ambassador, and they hit it off. A large picture of a World War II general dominated his office. Jason knew some history about the man and spoke knowingly of him.

The ambassador, who had served under the general, was delighted. "Anything we can do to make your stay more pleasant and comfortable, we will," he said enthusiastically.

That set the tone for the rest of Jason's stay. The cultural affairs and public affairs officers, who were in attendance, took note. Ever afterward, they were obsequious in inventing small pleasantries. And these actually increased after his successful recital at the ambassador's residence.

It was called a representational event and seemed to be part of a familiar package: If a post agreed to host you, it was obligatory to play at the residence if the ambassador requested it. The problem was that you never knew about the quality of the piano. But the food was good, and you would meet a variety of people, though you would probably never see them again. It was, above all, an excuse for the ambassador to invite the cream of society in order to increase his cultural contacts. And they all came to his palatial estate that evening to hear Jason play. The piano was adequate for the room and the Mozart sonata came off particularly well.

Afterward, there was the usual sit down dinner in a splendid banquet room with servants, cigars, and Cognac. The ambassador was resplendent in his red-and-black smoking jacket. Jason observed the others as well, and decided that Uruguayans were a somber, serious lot, rather self-sufficient, and not very demonstrative.

There was a certain greyness about Montevideo and an overall air of detached chaos. He would see more of the country the next day since the embassy had scheduled a sight-seeing trip into the interior. By going with the cultural affairs officer, Jason would get the equivalent of a professional tour guide. The Foreign Service were all schooled in the history and culture of the country where they were posted. The driver would be a foreign national who spoke fluent English. These were locals, hired by the embassy, and indigenous to the country, who could serve as translators as well as a resource for contacts.

"Uruguay has a population of three million, with half of it residing in Montevideo," said the officer.

That's the way it began as the car pulled out from the hotel early that morning.

Jason interrupted, telling about the smoked ham he'd just had for breakfast.

The officer looked bilious. "I couldn't eat that," he said in a wispy voice. "I'm a vegetarian." It was a moment before he looked out the window again. "Taken away from the Indians by the Spanish, it has struggled between autocracy and democracy for two hundred years since independence."

Jason wondered what a vegetarian ate for breakfast.

"Uruguay is close to Argentina in culture and attitude and broke away its boundaries only in the last century."

They were in a fast lane, leaving the city.

"Uruguayans can be haughty and extremely self-confident, unlike Argentineans. They perceive the future as the past, since things were better during the latter."

They drove along the inland bay of the Río de la Plata, away from the ocean. The Foreign Service Officer continued as though reading from a teleprompter. Jason was reminded of travel films the public-school system used to show when he was a boy.

"They prefer glory to suffering and have achieved sophistication through adherence to a predominantly French aesthetic."

They finally arrived at their destination—a provincial village named Colonia. There was not a great deal there, except the old Spanish section charmingly situated by the bay. They walked around a bit, then went to the city hall to meet the mayor.

The building was opulent and out of character with the modest simplicity of the town. They were shown into a room with high ceilings, flags, and big chairs lavishly upholstered in red. The mayor and his cabinet were sitting there, slightly drunk from lunch. They wore suits but had taken their ties off. Each of the six men smoked cigars and were dropping their ashes on the plush carpet. The cultural affairs officer began to speak Spanish with a thick American accent. He introduced himself, then Jason and finally the foreign national. The mayor broke into a broad grin that revealed missing teeth. He tried to get up but couldn't. When he fell back into his chair, ash from the cigar dropped into his lap. He tried to speak, but his voice came out in grunts.

The cultural affairs officer moved around the table and stood next to a flag. "This is the flag of Colonia," he said. "You will notice it has a very poignant logo."

The mayor's cabinet began to grunt together and at each other.

"Two lions on each side of a beautiful temple. Both animals poised, as predators ready to devour the temple." The officer pointed to them. He looked pallid and thin next to the well-fed men at the table.

Someone on the mayor's left grunted something and the others began to snicker.

"The lions, each in a different color, represent both Spain and Portugal, the two colonial powers that have held the city in the past."

The snickering at the table turned into laughter.

"Above this is fire, a weapon the colonial powers used against the colonists, and above this—"

Now it was raucous. The mayor's face was pinched. He squealed like a hyena.

Jason turned to the foreign national. "What's so funny?"

"Very difficult to translate."

The din increased, and one of the men started to pound the table.

"A Phoenix rising from the ashes..." The officer's voice trailed off.

"Try to translate whatever in the hell it is." Jason almost shouted at the foreign national.

"All right, it's something like this. One of the men at the table said that the cultural affairs officer looks like a mouse fart."

The next morning while he was packing to leave for the airport, the phone rang. "The deputy chief of missions would like to see you before you leave. Please stand outside the hotel, and a car will pick you up in five minutes." The heavily accented voice left no room for reply.

This was someone Jason had not yet met. The deputy chief of missions was just behind the ambassador in importance and wedged between him and the public affairs officer in the pecking order.

A dark-blue Chrysler was already at the main entrance. Besides the driver, there was a passenger in the back who slouched low. The driver left the engine running and got out to open the door on the passenger side. Jason slid into the back-seat, feeling like he was part of an old B movie. The car drove off... but not far.

"So what's Harry Cone up to?" The passenger took a drag from his cigarette. Jason could see a broad face with a large mustache under a felt hat, and soft hands that had never seen manual labor. A thirty-year veteran, he figured.

"You were his piano teacher, right? What's he up to? What's the atmosphere like back there in Washington?"

"About as bad as you could imagine," said Jason, playing it for all it was worth.

There was silence as the man blew smoke out of the corner of his mouth. Then more silence. Jason thought this film needed a better director.

"I may go back, and I may not," said the officer. "I don't have to. I could take another post down here or in Spain. Once you're down here, you can get a job anywhere on the continent. It's called the Vaseline circuit; you just slide around. I never liked it back there at the agency anyway. Especially with what I hear about this guy, Cone."

"Really?"

"Oh, c'mon, we can talk frankly. I hear you were even fired

once. Anyway, you never heard what I just said. And if you did, then I'll deny I ever said it." The man chuckled, then started to cough.

So did Jason. The car was filling up with smoke. "Do you think you could open the window a little?"

"Someone's liable to take a shot at you," said the officer, opening another pack of cigarettes.

The flight back to Brazil was long. This time, he was going to the city of Belo Horizonte, in the southeastern region of the country. A large city of several million, it was built on several hills and was surrounded by mountains. Brazil was bigger than the United States if you didn't include Alaska and Hawaii; that was the only memorable thing the over-achieving foreign national told him after he arrived.

"Please, let me brief you on your schedule right here, sir, because there is so much to do. Your bags won't be down for another moment anyway." The man had the routine Latin appearance of slicked-down, black hair and a mustache, and literally danced toward his briefcase. He pulled out some papers.

"I know a little bit about my schedule already," said Jason, trying to calm him down. "It was cabled to me. And since I don't have anything till tomorrow afternoon, why don't we postpone the briefing until the morning?"

Jason got to see a bit of the city those first couple of days, but most often he was carted off to whole series of newspaper interviews. He was also accompanied by photographers at his practice sessions, and there were television camera crews by his side at inappropriate times. But it was fun to be treated as a celebrity.

Jason's hotel was not great, but the accommodations had been included in a package deal, along with the concerts. So he took his dinners at the hotel restaurant every night and didn't worry about having to pay for them; everything was included. And the immense publicity he had generated made him interesting to other people. The maître d' always fussed over him by giving him a table by the window or out on the balcony. There he could look out on the mix of classical and contemporary architecture that made up the city.

He gave concerts on three successive nights at the Sesiminas complex, a hall that seated one thousand people.

"The entire venture is an experiment," the foreign national told him. "The branch post wants to bring a new kind of public into the concert world—the workers or blue-collar types. So we will experiment with price adjustments."

After the last concert, Jason buttonholed him backstage. "Why were there only twenty-five people on the first two nights, and tonight it looks like there were over a thousand?"

The foreign national smiled. "Because tonight was the free concert."

He had to give one more performance in a charming eighteenth-century village called Sabará, about twenty kilometers outside of Belo Horizonte. He was tired the day of the concert and needed to rest. He wanted to go to the hall at the last minute, but that was a problem with the branch post. There were not enough cars available to take him to the hall that late. Instead, he would have to leave three hours early.

"You can rehearse during the extra time," said the foreign national.

"I don't want to rehearse."

"Well, anyway, there is a very comfortable dressing room where you can relax."

When they arrived, Jason found a four-hundred-year-old Elizabethan theater with three tiers in the balcony. He saw a small grand piano on the stage but did not try it. It was too small to even worry about; no one would be able to hear it. He was too tired to be disappointed, anyway. He just wanted to rest.

"Show me the dressing room," he said to anyone listening.

He was taken downstairs into the basement of the theater. Four hundred years of cold dampness had made it forlorn. The dressing room was only a cubicle with low-hanging, mismatched wooden beams and a stone floor. There was a table, a stool, and a nail on the door. That was all, and that's where he waited, walking off some steam. He took a long time to change into his tuxedo. That would kill some time. But certainly not enough.

When the moment for the concert arrived, Jason's back was sore from sitting on the stool. He climbed the stairs with a slight stoop and walked behind the curtains. The stagehand had only one eye and had the habit of turning his head to the side when he looked at someone. He did this when nodding at the pianist to walk on.

Jason took the plunge and walked through the curtains onto the stage, but as the applause started, his last composed thought was of a flounder. He tried to fix his attention on the first piece he would play... until he took a few steps. The stage seemed tilted, like a bad dream. Everything dipped downward toward the audience. He had the feeling that if he had skates on, he would slide into the first row. The piano was sitting at a cockeyed angle, like it had an emergency brake on.

My God, he thought. *I could fall off.* He sat down, trying to get used to it. The angle was so sharp that the bass part of piano was higher than the treble side. He started with a Mozart sonata and watched his hands go downhill as he went up the keyboard. It was confusing. He did the best he could and brought the concert to a close with a dizzying piece that ran up and down the keyboard. His brains were scrambled.

Afterward, there was the usual reception, though not in the

theater. It was the secretary of culture for the region of *Minas Gerais* who offered to drive him there.

"He says it would be a great honor," the foreign national translated. "And I think it would be good public diplomacy to accept."

Jason got into the car with the other dignitaries, and the chauffeur drove fifty feet before the car stopped again. The reception was next door.

The following morning, he awoke limp from exhaustion. His tour was over, and he wondered if he had the energy to get to the airport for his flight back to the United States.

His plane ride to Miami seemed short, but the airport was crowded. There were long lines going through customs and he was in danger of missing his connection to Washington. The agents were looking for drug smugglers. Suddenly, he thought of his diplomatic passport. It might be good for something after all. He started walking toward the VIP clearance area. As he passed alongside the snakelike column of people waiting in line, a man in a wide-brim Panama hat and flower-print shirt said, "Hey, weren't you on *Meet the Washington Press* last month? Boy, you were great!"

Another piped up, "Atta boy, stick it to 'em!"

People started murmuring. A woman in a red satin pants suit

clapped, and other people joined in. Jason smiled, walking faster until he got to the booth at the gate. The federal agent smiled as he stamped his passport. Jason thought it was a good thing Harry Cone had not seen all this, or he'd get fired again. Harry didn't like to be upstaged by an underling. He had a sinking feeling. He was going back to all of that? Then another thought occurred to him: how different the rest of the country was from Washington.

The plane came in low over the Washington Monument and Fourteenth Street bridge. He was home again. Or was it home? He felt like a transient, but that was Washington: temporary, artificial, the dramatic, makeshift life of a political appointee—up, down and around. His heart sank. Rio suddenly seemed very far away.

CHAPTER EIGHT

*H*arry's fingers slid in and out of the black and white keys. He was doing a pattern of notes that belonged to a piece Jason had taught him years ago. He preferred to play it on the dummy keyboard where there was no sound. It was less confrontational to his ego than the mess he made of it on a real grand. His imagination filled with thoughts of being the greatest pianist in the world and that the étude he was playing was flying by at a dizzying speed. It wasn't, but the car was. Trees and foliage disappeared in the window frame like the flickering of a film as the car sped down rustic Rock Creek Parkway.

Harry's arms moved up and down the silent keyboard, his inner ear producing sounds heard only in the private sanctum of his imagination, until he remembered something Jason had told him: to lead with his arm going up the keyboard like a violin bow. He stopped abruptly. "Damn it! I have to have him give me a piano lesson." But how could he do that if he was going to fire him? Now would be the best time. It was over two months since the incident, and Harry figured people had probably forgotten. Jason wouldn't have support in the country anymore, and his firing might even go unnoticed. Something had to be done. After all, he had embarrassed Harry on *Meet the Washington Press*. Millions of people had heard Jason's disparaging remarks, and Harry could not allow someone like that to survive. Moreover, he called the president a "robot in a suit." And there were the jokes that Jason told which caused the president to embarrass himself in the East Room. Of course, Harry had told some jokes, too, but Jason could be more easily blamed since the president had laughed harder at Jason's jokes. After that came the debacle. Harry got rankled again. Maybe the president had bad taste in jokes. He looked out the window and decided they could all lose their jobs.

The car made an exit onto Connecticut Avenue and then down Sixteenth Street. The city was teeming with traffic, ambulance sirens, and pedestrians. As they came closer to the White House, people seemed to have more decorum, to wait more appropriately for a change of light; many had briefcases.

Harry struggled with the conflict. Should he cut Jason loose? That would be easy. There was only one thing that kept his vengeance in check: if he fired him, he would never get another piano lesson.

The car went through the gate, without being stopped, and onto the black, circular driveway of the North Portico of the White House.

Harry had a brainstorm. He would let the president of the United States decide.

The walk through the old federalist corridors was getting easier. He knew where he was going and was no longer in awe of the place. Marine guards saluted, and Harry loved it. He could still intimidate people. The doors to the oval office were opened with another salute.

"Thank you, son," he murmured to the adjutant.

The president looked up with his reading glasses. "Harry... What's the good word?"

"A man said his girlfriend wasn't very bright. She once stared at a can of orange juice for twenty minutes because it said 'concentrate.'"

The president laughed but not excessively. He turned serious. "Harry, my poll numbers are down. Ever since the East Room incident... You know, when I was down on my hands and knees."

Harry seized the moment. "You mean when that kid, Jason Angeletti, told you those jokes. He should have kept his mouth shut."

The president's eyes widened. "I don't blame him. He's funny as hell!"

Harry scowled.

"In fact, I never met anybody that funny. Bring him around for lunch sometime. We'll have a grand old time."

Jason dragged himself across the courtyard to his office. It was his first day back, and he thought of Marilyn. He had tried to put her out of his mind, and until now that had not been a great challenge, which surprised him. It was funny how being out of Washington made everything go away, all the anxiety and stress. He thought of the controversy before he left. Was the crisis past? It was already several months since he had appeared on *Meet the Washington Press*. Were the "long knives" still out, or had his time away mitigated any danger?

He sighed as he pressed the code on the security panel. The buzzer sounded, and he walked in and around the corner to his office. His secretary gave him a cheery "Welcome back!" There were fresh flowers on his desk and a pile of messages from TV networks and news shows, all wanting him to appear on their programs. The phone rang, and the secretary came in.

"It's Bill Barron from the director's office. I guess you're in the swim already."

He had never heard that expression before and thought about it as he picked up the phone.

Barron's sharp edge broke his rumination. "Jason, you are not to go near any of those news shows, got it?"

"I suppose so."

"Now, here's the director."

Jason straightened as the call was being transferred to a speakerphone. He heard a distant voice ask: "Is he on the line?" Then some squawking and a voice sounding like an old transatlantic shortwave broadcast.

"This is the chief. I have a significant request to make."

Jason wondered if this was the moment when Harry might ask for his resignation.

The director measured his words carefully. "I need a piano lesson."

"What?"

"I'll repeat. I need a piano lesson!"

"I'm not sure that's prudent."

"Whaddya mean?"

"We already went through that 'piano teacher' business... the Kiddiegate scandal when I got fired. I would hate to revisit that in the press."

"I don't give a damn!" Harry's voice was rising. "What's really important are my arms. I'm not sure they're moving in the right way when I go up the keyboard."

There was an uncomfortable silence.

"Look, boy, I'll make you a deal. If you give me a piano lesson, I'll take you to lunch with the president."

Jason drove to Harry's secluded house in Northwest Washington. He had never been there and got the directions from the front office. Security stopped him at the gate but already had his name; he didn't have to show any identification. He parked in the circular driveway and stayed a moment behind the wheel, thinking about his predicament. He had avoided giving Harry lessons. It was a mystery why Harry was so attached to them in the first place. He never improved.

The director was already at the door in a silk robe and slippers, so Jason got out of the car. He entered the house with his feet sinking pleasurably into a plush carpet. Harry escorted him into the living room where the piano stood; there would be no tour of the house.

Jason immediately opened the music sitting on the rack of the piano. It was the *Fantaisie Impromptu* of Chopin. "My God!" he said, looking it over. "Those are my markings from ten years ago."

Harry turned on a tape recorder.

"Are you sure we should record this?" Jason remembered the trouble Harry brought down on himself by tape-recording everybody else.

"Why not?" he answered, as if in a courtroom. "You're here in agreement."

Jason thought Harry would probably add this tape to the dozens of others he had taken during those five years Jason taught him.

It seemed long ago now, but for Harry, there was no cessation of time; it was a continuum.

As he began to play, Jason realized why. The piece had not improved in a decade. "Play the melody so that it sings more in the right hand."

"Why? There aren't any words." Harry's head swaggered.

"Make your hands sing."

"Boy, that would be a trick! What would do you do for an encore?"

"And here, after the double bar, your fingers have to articulate crisply in the right hand."

"Sounds like a chicken wing."

It was the same old thing. Only a few people besides Harry thought Harry was funny, and Jason wasn't one of them. Jason tried one more thing. He pointed to one of the measures. "And here it should sound more like a conversation between two people. Bring out one voice, then the other."

Harry grinned. "That's why I haven't spoken to my wife in three weeks. I don't want to interrupt her."

Jason closed the sheet music. "These suggestions that I've made should help the music take shape." He wanted out of there and got up to leave.

Harry looked deflated until he remembered who was still in charge. "Hey, you have to show me how to use my arms going up the keyboard!"

Jason doubled back, took the knob of Harry's elbow and moved it back and forth. "As long as this stays ahead of your hand, you're in business."

The lesson was over. As they walked to the door, Harry made a quick side trip to the kitchen and opened the refrigerator. "I want you to have some leftover stuff."

Jason was curious. A present from Harry Cone?

Harry took out a pear-shaped object, wrapped it in tinfoil, and gave it to Jason, bidding him, "Goodbye, friend."

As he walked to the car, Jason opened the tin foil. It was, in fact, a pear—ice cold and brown with age. He took a bite and threw it to the curb.

Good to his word, Harry arranged a luncheon with the president the very next week. A limousine picked Jason up in front of the agency. Harry was already in the backseat with the dummy keyboard on his lap. He would try to squeeze every bit of piano advice out of Jason over the stretching city blocks.

They discussed mostly technique: the physicality of playing with its proper movements. As they approached a red light, Jason took his left hand and placed it over Harry's right to show him the correct position in playing an arpeggio. A truck driver pulled up and peered down into the backseat of the limo. Disgusted at the sight of two men's hands touching, he honked his horn and gave them the finger.

The car pulled up to the southwest gate of the White House. Both doors of the backseat were opened by marine attendants. Harry returned a salute. Jason dared not.

Once inside, they rounded their way through the ground floor to the West Wing. Harry started to take a detour to show Jason the White House Steinway in the East Room but changed his mind when he looked at his watch. They walked past the cabinet room to the door to the oval office just off the Roosevelt Room. It was open. Harry walked in, but Jason hesitated.

Harry's voice rang out. "I just had a piano lesson in the car.

My teacher says my fingers are like lightening; they rarely strike the same spot twice."

There was laughter. Then the president asked, "Where is he?"

Jason stuck his head in. It seemed comfortable, like a living room. Sofas were arranged in front of the fireplace, and light came streaming through the beveled glass windows. The president sat at an ornate desk in front of the windows, with the Washington Monument rising in the background.

"Jason, do sit down. They're going to bring us lunch." The president took off his reading glasses.

An aid came from the kitchen to set up three TV trays. Another followed with soup, sandwiches, and soft drinks.

The president gestured toward the food. "Dig in, fellows." He chose the TV tray in front of the sofa, motioning for the other two to sit opposite him. "That's a great little program you've got, Jason." He dropped some crackers in his soup. "It's had tremendous impact. I remember the Caribbean thing." He looked at Harry. "What was the country that we saved down there?"

Harry searched his memory. "The one that makes all those baskets." He had been on a cruise to Aruba but couldn't recall the names of any other islands.

The president examined his sandwich. "How many pianists have you sent out so far, Jason?"

"Uh… just two, sir."

"What! This administration has been in place for two and a half years, and you've only sent out two!"

Jason froze.

"What a shame." The president shook his head. "We'll have to increase your budget. Harry, I want these pianists spread around the world!"

Harry nodded vigorously. "A lot of bang for the buck, especially when you compare it to the cost of an aircraft carrier. Speaking of cost, do you know why Jewish women like circumcised men? They can't resist anything with ten percent off."

The president laughed loudly, then looked at Jason. "Well, what have you got to say?"

"Thanks for your confidence, sir. I'll put the extra money to good…"

"No, I mean, do you have a joke for me?"

"A joke, sir?" Jason looked around the room, hoping his eyes might light on something that would trigger his memory. He noticed the half-eaten refuse on Harry's plate. "A woman came running out of her house chasing the garbage truck down the street yelling, 'Is it too late for the trash?' The driver said, 'No, jump in!'"

Harry's face darkened. It was another one of his jokes. Why should someone else get the credit?

The president almost spit out his Diet Coke. The laughter moved up to his shoulders which started to rise and fall rhythmically. He had trouble catching his breath. Tears meandered down his cheek. He gained enough breath to let out a howl and banged his hand down for emphasis, but the tin TV tray tipped off its legs, spilling everything on the carpet.

A secret service agent came running in. "Are you all right, sir?"

The president was doubled up on the sofa. The words came out in spasms. "Oh… my… god… he's… funny!"

The agent turned to the other two. "Gentlemen, I think that will be all for today."

The next morning, Jason came into his office with new purpose. He was determined to get his program moving again with no less than the president of the United States behind him. But now that he had to send more musicians out, he would need more staff. After Marilyn and his program coordinator had quit, all he had left was his secretary. He thought about going through the hiring process again for two new employees, but it was overwhelming. He decided to short-circuit the process. He would transfer someone laterally at the same grade level for an indeterminate period of time.

Bliss Fernmalvaison was a GS-12 level career employee. She had not always been career and, in fact, was a significant political appointee when serving as Mel Robespere's assistant. But when Mel was fired as deputy director of the whole agency, Bliss was quietly moved into a lifetime career slot as a reward for loyal service. But she was not happy with just job security. There was a yearning for the lost dominions of power that she had under her mentor.

Lacking real authority or power in her new life, she continually gravitated to those who did. Aided by tiny, perfectly formed teeth, a turned-up nose, and eyelashes meticulously applied to accentuate the smooth innocence of her face, Bliss was also hampered by her enormous bulk. She no longer looked like the young woman in the picture she provided on her résumé. That was taken years ago by the in-house journal of a senate office building with the caption "just another Washington babe." She had worked, at the time, for a senator. When he sexually harassed her, she gave into his demands but later retaliated by leaking an apocryphal story to his hometown newspaper that resulted in his defeat for reelection the next year.

"Jason, you need another program coordinator since the other one left. And I know you've begun to advertise on those stupid government bulletin boards because you have to. But honestly, most of the people that are going to apply at that level are going to have toys in the attic." Bliss's voice was soft like a child's.

Jason thought it curious that those caressing tones came from such a mountain of flesh. "I want you to take someone that's really good. She's a friend of mine that's on the outside right now, working in an embassy on Massachusetts Avenue. You'd have to pull strings to bring her in quickly, but she'd be loyal to you, and it would be wonderful to have her in the office. Only you could do this; only you are powerful enough. Everybody else would get hung up in channels."

Jason ignored the Washington-style flattery, but the idea of doing it quickly appealed to him. "I'd have to see the associate director of Administration and Personnel. He's a presidential appointee, so I might be able to speak to him directly."

"Nate Hinchmin's gone, you know. Harry Cone fired him, so there's a new guy up there now."

"Do you know anything about him?"

Bliss started to feel important. "He was a bank executive in California. He's tied into the White House because he crafted the vice president's environmental speeches during the campaign. But what you really need to know is that he has a hair-trigger temper, a hair weave, and falls asleep a lot. His staff is infuriated because he can't remember in the afternoon what he's been told in the morning, so they think he either drinks or he's narcoleptic."

"Bliss, is this the kind of stuff you did for Mel Robespere when you worked for him?"

"He couldn't make a decision without me. Those were my happiest days. I knew just what to do for him. I even slid memos under the door of his private toilet for him to sign. Then I'd have to walk them around for the other signatures because the secretaries wouldn't touch them." Bliss wrinkled her nose and giggled. Her great weight was concealed under a loose-fitting, one-piece outfit that swept everything nearby.

On a Wednesday afternoon, Jason made his way upstairs to the office of the associate director. It was a large office, befitting Winston Waldrip's rank. Jason had been in many of them. They all seemed the same, with the panoramic view and photographs of political celebrities on the wall.

As Winston moved out from behind his desk, Jason observed that certain wooden CEO-type in his late fifties with a slight stoop. He also had a way of pivoting his whole body when only his head and neck needed to turn.

"I've heard all about you, Jason. You're a celebrity around here. I've also heard about your successful program and understand the director has been personally interested in it. You are to be commended for a very bright idea." The associate director guided Jason to a cushioned chair. "In this age of confrontation, we must have communication. And you have accomplished that, I might add."

"Thank you." Jason was looking for a hook to begin the conversation.

"The experience of prudent judgment and insightful problem solving is what breeds success." Winston pointed his finger for emphasis. "You have to arrive quickly at the right decisions, and that way, you develop sharp instincts. You really need to become the sum of all that in order to succeed."

"Right." Jason tugged at his ear. "Listen, Mr. Waldrip, there's someone I'd like to hire for my office, but I have to bring them in from outside the agency. Since that process can get lengthy and complicated, I'd like to find a way to expedite it."

"A personnel action, huh? What's the grade level?"

"GS-eight, sir."

"That's not very high. What's this person's name?"

"Maxine Largesse."

"Largesse… How'd she get a name like that? Is she big or something?"

"Well, names don't necessarily mean—"

"You've never met her, huh?"

"No, but I have an excellent recommendation."

"Where is she now?"

"She's at an embassy downtown. I do have a phone number."

"But if you don't know what she looks like, how do you know that's her on the phone?"

"Well, you can't see people on the phone anyway."

"Right, but I don't want to bring anybody in here that we haven't seen at all. Director of security is one of my responsibilities. Where will she be going if she finds this building?"

"To my office."

"Where's that?"

"In this building."

"Where in this building?"

"Downstairs."

"How many people are down there?"

"You mean, downstairs?"

"Yeah."

"Depends on how many people are in the lobby."

"I mean, how many do you have working for you?"

"There are four people in the office, counting myself."

"And without you, how many are there?"

"Three."

"That's good. You get more than that, and it can be a problem. Look at the IRS for God's sake!"

The conversation seemed to end, and it was uncomfortably quiet. Winston peered intently, giving the impression of silent energy. "Listen," he said finally. "If you can assure me that the next time you call this woman, that it's really her at the other end of the phone, then I'll sign off on this." He got up as he finished his sentence. This was a sign that the meeting was over.

Jason always thought it was a little cold, the way meetings with high-level people ended. In such instances, one never said goodbye. And it seemed too servile to say "thank you," especially if you didn't get what you wanted. Since he felt awkward in leaving without any acknowledgement, he adopted a routine of just sauntering toward the door. That was the drill, and it made him feel better to know exactly what he was going to do. But as he was walking out, he thought to ask Winston something else. When he turned, the associate director was already seated at his desk. At first it appeared that he was reading, but his head was farther down than necessary, his chin resting against his chest. And he was snoring.

Maxine Largesse proved even heftier than Bliss. When Jason watched the two move through the office—especially side by side—he couldn't help thinking of two overstuffed sofas gliding through the air. These were not sophisticated women, but they knew the ways of Washington. And in some quarters, this passed for worldliness, even polish. The thought of the two of them in the office instead of Marilyn made him cheerless, but then he smiled. It was amusing to compare them: glamour versus earthbound obesity. Was this just part of the dramatic changing of happenstance so typical of Washington, or had he done something wrong?

Bliss had taken to wearing a giant pink jumpsuit in the office that zipped up the front. She acted like she was in her own living room, frequently taking off her shoes. The carpet felt better on her stocking feet, she explained. But there was also trouble with her lower extremities. That had been turned over to the care of a podiatrist. The previous week she had asked about sick leave. "Jason, do you know about that regulation that says you can be out of work for two days without a doctor's excuse? I'd like you to extend that to three. And on Thursdays, I'd like to leave at three thirty without having to take any sick leave because I've got an appointment with my psychiatrist. It would just stress me out to have to get docked in pay for that appointment since it's the government that's making me crazy anyway. And on Fridays, I have to see my primary care physician for allergy shots and hypoglycemia. I should leave at three because of all the traffic. And then, my chiropractor expects me every other week. I know all of this sounds like a lot, but it keeps me going."

"Who pays for this?"

Bliss wrinkled her nose. "The government, silly. We've got the best health care insurance there is."

"I guess that's why Maxine feels she can smoke like a forest fire—all day long."

"I've told her to quit, but she won't. She's so grateful to you for having the whole office named as a designated area for smoking. We're lucky to be apart from the main building and make our own rules. I can't believe that we even have our own security system. Maxine and I are going to watch a movie this afternoon on the new office TV."

It was clear he had to instill discipline with the advent of more national auditions. He quickly put new procedures in place, using the same models as before but with more consultants traveling around the country as more artists were chosen. Before long, the office settled into a new rhythm, and the auditions took place over several months.

Meanwhile, Jason sent out offering cables to posts throughout the world. The program had enough credibility now that posts would sign up for a touring musician sight unseen. He decided to enhance the intercultural aspects by trying homestays for the artists. They would stay with local families to more embed them into the culture. It was a bone thrown to a particular element of the Foreign Service: the "culture vultures" who would be enthusiastic about the idea.

To his relief, everything had fallen into place. The only incident was when Maxine took an outgoing cable up to the secretariat, and her cigarette ashes burned a hole in the part about the pianist's itinerary. Otherwise, all the schedules had worked out, and soon the tours were in full swing.

When the evaluation cables started coming in, it was a clean sweep; they were exultant. And almost all of them used the same words: "astounding," "a smashing success," or "superlative." His secretary brought in more, but he didn't look at them. His star was rising again. Videos of his speeches at the congressional reception and the auditions themselves were even being played on television sets in the lobby. His role now was to simply oversee what had already been put in place and was working, but mistakes still had to be avoided and fires put out.

His secretary came in, her eyebrows raised. "It's a heads-up call from Italy."

Jason stared at the phone. He hated these kind of calls—unofficial complaints made in whispers. They were meant to ward off disaster. *Italy?* he thought. *That's Marvella Ludlow!*

Marvella Ludlow was a thirtyish, demure, assistant professor of piano at Elmira University in Butte, Montana. She had charmed the judges in the final round at the Library of Congress with a sonata by Schubert. During her agency briefings with the Foreign Service, she had impressed them, too, because of her willingness to please. She took all their names and afterward sent them gifts that were returned because of government restrictions.

"Mr. Angeletti, I'm an officer in the embassy here in Rome. Listen! You can't believe everything this dame has packed. It's costing the embassy a fortune to cart her around. And the *coup de grâce* was when we sent her up to Bologna by train in order to save airfare. She took seven hat boxes with her. Seven hat boxes on an Italian train!"

Jason tracked her down in a remote mountain village directly east of Naples called Monta Moura. There was a six-hour time difference and much confusion as the night clerk at the hotel strained to understand. The faulty overseas connection did not help. Finally, the clerk said, "*Si, si, Americana signora. Un momento, please.*"

A high-pitched voice broke in. "Hello?"

"Yes, this is Jason Angeletti in Washington. I've just been in touch with the American embassy in Rome, and they're complaining you've got too much baggage. I'll have to ask you to send some home now."

"But... I don't understand. I really don't have that much."

"That much? What about seven hat boxes?"

"What? I've only got one, and I couldn't get along without it."

"I have to tell you that this is the U.S. government calling, and you're costing the taxpayers needless sums of money. We've been watching you all through your travels, and we know exactly what you've got. I'm getting phone calls about you, and soon there will be official cables."

"My God," she said desperately. "I don't understand. I've always been a good American. I even voted for the president. Why are they watching me?"

"That doesn't matter. Just pack everything you don't need, and we'll have the embassy ship it home in a diplomatic pouch."

"But I really need everything. I really do!"

"Look, how many concert dresses do you have?"

"I don't have any."

"Why not?"

"Because I don't play concerts."

"You played one last night."

"The hell I did! Listen, who is this? Give me the name again!"

Jason suddenly felt limp. He wanted to hang up but stammered out his name almost inaudibly, hoping she wouldn't hear.

"Well, I'm not the person you want to talk to. There's another American woman down the hall, and I think she's a pianist. I'm going to get her right now."

After several minutes, the same woman returned. "Sir?"

"Yes."

"Miss Ludlow says she doesn't take calls after ten."

The evaluation cable came in from Italy and, to Jason's relief, was superb. Apparently Marvella's art overrode any inconvenience she might have caused the embassy. He ordered his staff to make short synopses of all the evaluations, so they could be sent around to the press section and the heads of the geographic areas. It would be good public relations.

He was relaxing in his office, going over some correspondence with the radio tuned to the classical music station. Beethoven's Seventh Symphony had just started. The intercom buzzed, and he noticed it was in the same key as the symphony.

"It's Marvella Ludlow on the line. This time it's from Copenhagen."

He picked up the receiver.

"Jason, I think you should eliminate the homestays." Marvella's voice was low.

"Could you speak up, please?"

"Get rid of the homestays!" she shouted.

"What happened?"

"The post asked me if I'd like to stay in a castle with some aristocrat. It sounded fine. I've never been in a castle and—"

"What happened?"

"This Danish count sent his family and staff away for the weekend and then chased me around the castle."

Someone banged on her door.

"Do you hear that? Honest to God, Jason, I've had nothing to eat for three days because I locked my door and wouldn't go downstairs! I finally opened the window and stopped a street vendor. He threw three sandwiches up before one finally hit the window. I had to pay for all three of them."

"Have you told the embassy?"

"Yes, and they're not helping."

He put a call through to the cultural attaché.

"We can't touch him," Jason was told. "This guy is slated to be prime minister."

Jason looked out the window. Marvella called back.

"It's okay now, Jason. I called the police. There's no more banging on the door."

"Did they talk to him?"

"No, they just put him in their little wagon."

Jason waited for days, but the embassy never called. Finally, the press section called from the fifth floor. Stuart Stadler was excited again. His words came out with the rapidity of a machine gun. "You did it again! Wow, the Smithsonian ought to study you! How do you do it?"

"Do what?"

"Denmark! They nailed this sleezebag, and the prime minister of Denmark wrote our president, thanking him for that opportunity. Seems this guy was under investigation for financial corruption but was too powerful to go after. He could have become prime minister, but the police complaint from Marvella Ludlow tipped it over the edge. After it hit the papers, they were able to throw the book at him. They're saying it was the Musical Emissary Program that saved the day."

That month, Jason made the cover of the agency magazine again. His interview rankled some of the political appointees because they would have preferred that he pumped the reelection of the president. Instead, he said that he would hold no more auditions since a new president might not continue the program. The musicians chosen from the auditions in one administration might never be sent out in the next. The reference to a new president was an insinuation that this president might well be defeated. The campaign season was beginning. Things were polarized and serious.

The phone rang. It was Shelley Fatachawada.

"Boy, you are somethin' else. You break all the rules, and you come out on top."

"Is that a compliment?"

"I dunno. I gave up tryin' to figure you out."

"I'm just trying to get through."

"Get through? You should be grabbing everything you can get! You may never come this way again." She lowered her voice. "Jason, now that the campaign's underway, it's clear to me that the president may not win reelection. Every time I turn on the television, they're showing that damn tape of him in the East Room on his hands and knees. He looks like a yo-yo, and you're standing right next to him. Everybody in the country has seen it, and some of our friends in the agency are blaming you."

"I'm just a scapegoat."

"Well, I'm not even supposed to be talking to you, but you've got this great program, and we need it."

"What do you want?"

"Jason, we all know what a great job Harry Cone has done for this agency and for the president… right?"

Jason imagined Shelley pumping her arm in the air.

"Lurking Autos is giving Mr. Cone an award, and he'll probably give them one, too. I want to do it up big. I've got all the big guns coming down from Detroit. Harry deserves a tribute, and besides, I'm going to hit him up for job placement somewhere in the private sector if we get screwed in the election. This could be our last hurrah."

"What do you want from me?"

"Your program is the only thing he's got going. Everything else is at a standstill because of the election and all the bad press he's gotten. So we're going to highlight it! I want you to write talking points with all the good news, so I can give it to him for his remarks at the dinner."

"Why is Harry giving Lurking Autos an award?"

"Because of their support for your program."

"What support?"

"The're paying for this dinner."

"Am I invited?"

"I'm not sure. I don't know whether you personally are up or down with him right now. You're kind of a pariah. But he needs the Musical Emissary Program. Let me think about it."

Jason sent her the materials and the next morning got another call from Shelley.

"Listen, Jason! Now you gotta come to this thing. I just found out the die-rek-ta is going to talk about you."

"Shelley, I don't really want to be there anyway."

"You have to be there! Listen, don't act like a banana.

This'll be good for you and the program." She was out of breath. "I rented a limo that's a block long. I think it's the right way to do things. It's what the die-rek-ta would want. We can't go there looking like pikers. We gotta represent somethin'."

"And you want me to come along?"

"Damn right, Jason! You, me, and Gloria, my assistant. We're goin' in there like we're somebody. This is big! I just found out that senators and congressmen are coming... and journalists and a couple people from the president's cabinet and even powerful people from the opposing party!" Shelley was getting herself worked up. "We're gonna leave from downstairs at five forty-five p.m. tomorrow night, so set your watch. I don't want anything to go wrong."

The limousine was huge but old and creaky. Shelley climbed into the back seat with a large briefcase. Jason sat next to her while Gloria, a tall middle-aged blonde, settled in the jump seat. The soft leather and legroom gave the feeling of being in a living room. Shelley opened her briefcase and took out a sheaf of papers while the limo driver settled his foot on the accelerator. The car moved slowly from the curb like a boat leaving its slip. She looked at the papers and shook her head. Her hand returned down into the briefcase and beat against its leather sides like some trapped animal.

"Gloria," she shouted. "I can't find Harry's talking points. We gotta go back!"

The driver was easing around a corner when he braked. "We're so late now; we can't go back," said Gloria.

The driver accelerated.

"But Harry will be pissed." Shelley was frantic.

The limousine started to turn around in traffic.

"No, he won't," said Gloria. "He'll just do what he always does—call on Jason to speak."

The driver was halfway around when he changed direction again. Cars in both lanes started honking.

When they arrived at the gala, an agency photographer with flash bulbs took pictures of them exiting the car. The backdrop was the hotel, which sat with distinction on the wharf in the Georgetown area. Fashionable and powerful people were everywhere. They arrived one after the other in limousines, cabs, and black sedans. Jason recognized some from television.

The women were beautifully coiffed with blinding jewelry. Not all the men wore tuxedos. Many came fresh from work and felt they needed nothing more to set them apart.

Shelley Fatchawada was in her element as she worked the crowd in the gilded room. "Isn't this a wonderful program? A wonderful idea," she cooed from one cocktail huddle to another. "This was Die-rek-ta Cone's idea. He thought it up. It's his baby. Lovely to see you again."

Harry Cone came in, moving swiftly amongst the mostly taller pillars of power. Dispensing quick remarks here and there, he shook hands as if in a political campaign. Everyone schmoozed until the national public relations director for Lurking Autos clinked his glass. People began looking for their places at the different tables. The cocktail hour was over; it was time for the awards.

He moved toward the podium which had a Lurking Auto emblem draped over the front of it. "Ladies and gentlemen, I want to welcome everyone here. It is a very distinguished audience indeed. And now, without further ado, I will introduce to you the chief executive officer of Lurking Autos, Mr. Ronald Lurking."

A slight, balding man with glasses stood up from his chair and moved toward the podium. Jason thought he looked remarkably like the public relations director who had just introduced him.

Ronald Lurking was a descendent of the founder of the automotive industry and seemed calm and free from any immediate concerns. He was holding a plaque. "Ladies and gentlemen, as you can see, I have something in my hand. Written on it is the name of an esteemed person in this room. Indeed, besides the president, this is one of our most revered citizens. At least, we feel that way at Lurking Autos. Harry, let me ask you to come up here. I'd like to read this to you."

Harry didn't have far to go since he was already seated next to the microphone.

"Lurking Autos salutes Harry Cone." Ronald Lurking looked down at the plaque. "A man who has created opportunities for others by revitalizing the performing arts in this country through the creation of the Musical Emissary Program."

There was applause as Harry accepted the plaque. He adjusted the microphone downward. "Ladies and gentlemen, of all the awards that I've ever gotten in my long life, of all the honors…" Harry held out the plaque. "This… this is definitely the most recent." He grinned and searched the room for laughs.

There were few takers.

"Now, Mr. Lurking," he said. "I'd like to turn the tables and give you something to commemorate our appreciation of you at the ICCA."

There was a loud thud in the middle of the room as Shelley Fatchawada got up so quickly that her chair tipped over. She made a running start for the podium, carrying the plaque she had forgotten to give Harry. She tore the wrapping paper off as her posterior bobbed and weaved against chairs and tables and through impossibly narrow passageways. People pulled their chairs in tightly, but Shelley still got stuck twice on the way up. As she approached him, Harry grabbed the plaque as if it were a brass ring.

"To Lurking Autos," he said, holding it up. "In appreciation of the fine direction of its chief executive officer, Mr. Ronald Lurking, in revitalizing the performing arts in America through its support of the ICCA."

Shelley was taking the lengthier way back to her chair, along the circumference of the wall.

"I'd like to say some things now," said Harry, "about the Musical Emissary Program. Ms. Fatchawada, do you have my remarks?"

Shelley had made it back to her chair, still wheezing when she heard the question. She stood for a moment, her heart pounding in a way that punishes heavy people for moving too quickly. She waited, but there was nothing—no messages from within as to what she should do. She didn't have his remarks and looked at Harry like a helpless supplicant, not wanting him to explode at her in front of everyone. And then, her immaculately honed sense of survival made her think of Jason. She remembered what her assistant, Gloria, had said in the car. Slowly and without changing the position of her head, her eyes moved across the room and finally locked on Jason's. She looked quickly back at Harry and nodded in Jason's direction. Then, as if to cinch the deal, pointed to him.

Harry picked up the cue. "Well, I guess there's too much paper in the government anyway. You don't need me to read remarks when there's only one man who can really talk about this program, and that's Jason Angeletti. I picked him to run this program with the same confidence that I picked our president to run this country."

There was a gasp from the audience. Everyone knew Harry had raised exorbitant amounts for the president's campaign, but this was brazen, even for Washington. Harry knew, however, that people would be drawn to his remark because it smacked of power and confidence.

"So come on up here, Jason, and tell these people about the program."

Jason made his way up to the front. People studied his every move. Some allowed themselves to wonder if Harry's judgment of presidential timber might even extend to this young man.

"Ladies and gentlemen..." He stopped to sip some water from the glass on the podium. "Or maybe just plain 'folks.' That sounds better, doesn't it? Sometimes we get a little too stuffy around here."

The audience tittered.

"I'm supposed to tell you about the Musical Emissary Program. That's easy for me to do because it's based on a simple precept: find good people who work cheap, then use them as much as possible. That way, everybody wins. Is that exploitation? Not really. Classical musicians are always happy to work because there are few opportunities to work elsewhere. And if a performing artist doesn't perform, he or she dries up anyway. That's just the way they're wired. So we're saying to these artists, 'Uncle Sam wants you to do what you do best!' In return, they get credibility, a scrapbook of reviews, and a reason to live. And we get to disprove the myth that you have to be famous to be as good as the famous."

Jason peered into their faces.

"All of you here tonight are, by the standards of the world around us, very successful people. You have made the capitalist system work for you. And I am sure that you could list the ingredients for your success. It might be guts, drive, imagination, and discipline. Can you imagine having all those things and still not being able to succeed or even pay your bills? That's how tough it is in the field of classical music."

There was not a sound in the room.

"The irony here is that the government is sending people overseas to represent the United States in this Musical Emissary Program who are not making it in their own country, and they're succeeding overseas because they've finally been given a chance. We need art and beauty in our lives. We Americans can't just keep spending money without nourishing our soul, but unfortunately, that is the state of our culture. What can you do about it? Awareness! The next time you see or hear an artist, remember that they are as important to your life on this planet as the air you breathe."

There was silence as Jason sat down. Then the room burst into applause, and several people got to their feet.

Shelley Fatchawada watched with her mouth open. This guy just told everybody that all they cared about was money, and they gave him a standing ovation. Her eyes teared up as she contemplated the unfairness of it.

The evening was winding down. More people came to shake Jason's hand, then Harry Cone's. Even Harry walked over to Jason. There was a wistfulness in the air. Something new was emerging, a primordial ritual that arrived with every quadrennial coming.

"Well, boy," said Harry. "Whatever happens in the election, it's been a hell of a ride."

CHAPTER NINE

$\mathcal{N}$ovember came to Washington with a smoky-purple, Thanksgiving sky. The air was cold and dry, and the trees, bereft of any foliage, stood grey and knotted along the streets. Green colors had left as wind swept dead leaves by. It was election day, and the cycles of nature and politics were playing themselves out.

It is an American adage that "all good things must come to an end," and even the book of Ecclesiastes says, "For everything there is a season... a time to be born and a time to die." This remains true for good men and great, for the powerful and for those who own hardware stores. Metabolic decay heralds the end of the human condition, while public impatience can bring an end to a political administration. Early news projections showed the president being defeated in a landslide with both houses of Congress going to the opposing party. It was a debacle. Defenders of the administration became scarce, even among those who had been loyal. Little was said in the stinging aftermath, so overwhelming was the defeat.

The meaningful question in Jason's environment was not whether death would force men to do their ultimate thinking, but rather: Was there life after a federal agency?

There would be a new president, and it was axiomatic that this president would bring in his own people, as had every new administration since the beginning of the republic. Washington was in transition, like a soul departing its body. You could feel in the air that the patient was terminal, and that their affairs needed to be put in order.

Jason let himself into his office. His secretary, sensing the end, had already transferred to another job. Bliss and Maxine kept their own hours and, when there, circled him like vultures over a corpse. It was quiet—very quiet. There were no printers going, no machine sounds, and no phone calls. He could almost hear the traffic outside, which he had never noticed before. Then he heard the security buzzer, and the outside door opened.

Bliss walked in to the rustle of clothing. She was wearing a large housecoat. "Jason, you know how much I admire you and how much I appreciate you and—"

"What's on your mind?"

"Well, you're not going to be here much longer, and—"

"Come to the point."

"My evaluation is coming up. If you gave me an outstanding rating and then a promotion, I could head up this program after you leave. I'd take really good care of it, honest."

He smiled but said nothing. *Ludicrous*, he thought. *Bliss running a music program?* She couldn't even hum a Christmas carol.

The morning mail came. He opened one letter immediately because it was from the transition team of the new president. They thanked him for his service to the country and requested his resignation. Each political appointee had received one.

The phone rang.

"Jason? It's Marilyn Goodrump."

He took a breath. "It's been a while"

"I called to say goodbye... in case we don't see each other again."

There was an awkward silence.

"I mean, people do lose touch."

"Right!" he said.

"There was a party last night for all the political appointees."

"I wasn't invited."

"I'm sure you didn't expect to be. They're all in a panic... trying to get new jobs and all. What will you do?"

"I'm not in a panic. I have my music. They don't."

"But can that sustain you?"

"I'll be taken care of... somehow."

"Sorry it all ended. You could have been somebody in this town."

"I don't need this town to be somebody."

"Goodbye then, Jason."

Harry Cone pulled the collar up on his overcoat. The wind was harsh on the East Portico of the Capital as the president-elect placed his left hand on the bible and raised his right. The chief justice slowly intoned the oath, line by line. Each second brought Harry's world closer to an end. *How did it come to this,* he wondered, *the promise of another term gone up in a puff of ash.*

The new president gave a short inaugural address, then, accompanied by the chief justice, started his walk back into the Capitol, passing the old guard on his right. The former president rose slowly and applauded, along with his cabinet and sub-cabinet-level appointees seated behind him. Then the door to the Capitol closed.

Harry shuddered. He was on the outside now. There would be nothing more.

Jason was coming to his office for the last time to pack some things. It was a dreary, cold day as he carried boxes through the lobby. No one said anything. That was in keeping with no one even having called to say goodbye. He walked out into the courtyard toward his office. The security system was dismantled, so he was easily able to let himself in. It was quiet and dark, like a mausoleum. Bliss and Maxine had apparently already transferred to a new job. They lacked the graciousness to even tell him.

It was macabre as he flicked on the light and looked around, but the visitor's area seemed inviting, the only place still alive. Maybe it was the colors. He went over and sat for a moment, aware he had had little time to reflect over the years. Now he allowed himself that privilege. His eyes settled on Marilyn's office, then his own. Harry was right. It had been a hell of a ride. Who would believe any of it? A melancholy feeling swept over him, now that it was over. Everything had gone so fast that it was almost as though it had never happened. But he really did want out.

He decided against any more self-indulgence and went into his office. He took some pictures and his favorite pen and placed them carefully in a box, then the small radio in another. The phone rang. He wondered if it was Marilyn. Maybe she had more to say. He stared at it, finally picking it up on the fourth ring.

"Mr. Angeletti?"

"Yes."

"This is Chad Corbin. I'm the head of the transition team for the new president."

Jason was astonished. "I just sent you my resignation as per the instructions in your letter. All my colleagues did as well."

"Yes, but that's old news. Some of the president-elect's staff heard your speech at the Lurking Auto presentation. The reason I'm calling, sir, is because the president-elect would now like you to head up the entire agency under his administration. Will you accept?"

finis

ABOUT THE AUTHOR

John Robilette is an international concert pianist who has performed in 26 countries around the world including some of its major classical music venues. He has also recorded commercial CDs' of solo pieces as well as piano concerti with leading orchestras in Europe. Also now a SAG actor, he has had the lead or supporting roles in nine independent films, many of which were officially selected in film festivals around the Unites States and in Tokyo, Japan. He further wrote, directed and produced a 30-minute shot comedy film entitled, "My Piano Lesson." He holds a Master of Fine Arts degree from UCLA, a Doctor of Musical Arts from the Catholic University of America with earlier studies at the École Normale de Musique in Paris, France. Dr. Robilette has further served on the piano faculties of two universities and given master classes around the world. As a young man in 1981 he was asked to play a recital at the inauguration of President Ronald Regan. Subsequently, he was brought into the administration as a political appointee where he created and directed the Artistic Ambassador Program for the United States Information Agency from 1983-1989. This was an intercultural exchange program revolving around classical music which became popular in 63 countries around the world and was honored at the White House. The now defunct United States Information Agency was an executive agency that reported directly to the White House.